For all of the Peppermint Playbook series ladies. Thanks for making this Christmas magical.

The Holiday Assist

Taylor Epperson

Author's Note

Dear reader,

This book is a fun, holiday romcom. For the most part, it is light-hearted. If you like reading content warnings, continue with this letter. If not, head to the next page to start reading. As always, your mental health matters most, so if you aren't in the headspace to read a book that has anxiety representation, I totally get that. This book will be waiting for you another day.

Onto the content warnings:

Both characters deal with different types of anxiety. There is a panic attack on the page, and the other character helps them calm down.

There is also an ex that likes to hang around, but (possible spoiler) he's pretty harmless.

If you're still a little unsure, this book has fake dating, a guy who's head over heels in love with the female main character, and no third act break up.

Merry Christmas,

Taylor

Chapter 1

Juliet

The resort in Winterbrook is just as Christmassy and holiday-themed as the brochure promised it would be. My heart leaps in anticipation; having grown up with a dad who walked out on us and a mom who doesn't care for holidays means I never had the real Christmas experience. My mom is *the best* with everything else—she comes to every single one of my games and she makes dinner from scratch most nights, even when we're on the road with my team. But when it comes to Christmas, she has no interest in the holiday. Once I was a little older, my best friend's family took me under their wing and we'd hang out together, but her family doesn't really do Christmas either. Her parents are both professors, and academia was always more important than holidays. Family was everything, just not holidays.

But this year, it'll be a real Christmas celebration. I'm not with my team; there won't be any early morning drills unless I want to do them on my own. It'll just be me, my best friend, and her younger brother.

And all the athletes who are here for this charity event.

"This is it," my Uber driver says, stopping in front of a large white stone building that's covered from top to bottom in Christmas decorations. It looks like I've stepped into Santa's palace at the North Pole, or what I'd imagine he'd live in. You know, if he existed. There are turrets and lights and decorations in every direction. The only way I can think to describe it is *magical*.

"Thanks," I say. Climbing out, I notice that it's lightly snowing—the flakes barely visible since it's also sunny. Even though I grew up in Colorado, I could never figure out how that works. My driver grabs my duffel bag from the trunk as I pull out my phone and text Blair. She texted me a few minutes ago, telling me that they were close and that Parker was driving the rest of the way after a stop down the canyon.

ME

Just got here. I'll wait for you two if you're close before I check in.

BLAIR

We're like five minutes away, I think. We made it to Winterbrook and just need to find the resort.

Just look for all the minty things. This Mr. Mynt guy really takes his name seriously.

LOL. You must be in Christmas heaven.

I might be more excited if I didn't have to do all the athlete things.

> *eye roll emoji* It's for the children, J.
> Think of the children. The reason people
> are coming is because they want to
> meet you.

> I am not that famous.

> I beg to differ. You were called up to be
> on the U.S. Olympic team. You call that
> not famous?

I frown. This is one of those topics that I prefer to keep off limits. I may have been called up for the Olympic team, but I didn't go to the Olympics. Thinking of it still leaves a bitter taste in my mouth. How it all went down just left me feeling icky, which is why my manager suggested I be the one to come to The Mynt to Make a Difference charity event. It'll be good for my brand, she said. Mr. Mynt is the resort owner and just launched an athletic clothes brand, which is why he invited a bunch of athletes for his charity event to help raise money for his town of Winterbrook. But I'm not exactly sure what the funds will be used for—possibly the athletic program for the kids in town, but I could be wrong.

I'm just happy I don't have to spend Christmas alone and can leave the past year in the past. I've got to move on and be the best player I can be. This vacation is exactly what I need.

"Jules!" Someone calling my name pulls me out of my thoughts.

I turn to find Blair running toward me. Her arms fly around me. We've been best friends since first grade, but we don't see each other much these days.

She's a fancy hotshot lawyer in Denver, and I play soccer for a professional team in DC and the national team. We're both busy, but every time we see each other in person or talk on the phone, it's like no time at all has passed. We're just us again, falling right back into place.

"You made it!"

"I had to drive up to Loveland to pick up Parker, so that made the ride longer. I should have offered to pick you up from the airport."

I shake my head, laughing as I give her one more squeeze before releasing her. "And add another hour to your trip? I don't think so. The Uber was fine. My driver wasn't chatty, but he played all the best Christmas songs, so it was great."

She knows that I'm not much of a talker with strangers anyway. If we're friends, I become a completely different person, unguarded and carefree. But around everyone else? I'm closed off and focused on soccer. It's easier that way.

"I'm glad it wasn't too terrible. Parker was grumpy the entire time, then when we got to the canyon to get up here, he got all clammy. It was super weird," she says.

"Maybe he just doesn't like driving in the mountains?" I ask.

She grins, the smile reaching her eyes. "I'm pretty sure the closer we got, the more he realized that he's spending this break not stuck in his office at the school, and instead somewhere he'll have to be around people. He told me he packed three novels. Three. No way is he holing himself up in the room with a book. We're here for you, and I've been looking at that itinerary you sent over. It's going to be a busy week."

I take a deep breath. I wasn't even the one talking, but I'm out of breath. This is one of the things I love about Blair: she moves at one hundred miles an hour, non-stop. Parker's speed is probably closer to mine, but I'm not about to tell my best friend that. And I'm not going to tell her that I've got a thick fantasy novel tucked in the bottom of my duffel bag.

"All I really want is peppermint hot chocolate and some Christmas carols and maybe a sleigh ride."

Her eyes light up. "That's something the resort offers! Later this week."

"Fabulous. And I'm glad you two made it."

"We would have made it sooner if Parker weren't such a rule follower and hadn't driven exactly the speed limit. Plus, he got all weird, but I'm not going to let my little brother spend another holiday cooped up in his office prepping for another semester."

"I heard that," a deep male voice says from our right. I don't recognize it. How long has it been since I last saw Parker? Five years? Six? Usually, when I'm able to come to Colorado, I only hang out with Blair. The last time I saw him was probably when I was home for Christmas one year in college and he was still in high school. As I turn to face the voice—whom I can only assume is Parker, all grown up—I have to stop myself from openly gawking.

Long gone is the lanky teenage boy that I remember. The man standing before me—because he's all man now—has legs for days and thick thighs like he works out at

6

least semi-regularly, and unfortunately for me, thighs are my ultimate weakness. His form-fitting pants do nothing to hide his glorious muscles. He's in a loose tan cardigan and he's got those slutty little glasses like Jonathan Bailey had in that one movie.

Parker James has glasses. Ones that make him look like a hot professor I want to skip class for and make out with instead. My best friend's brother is hot.

Gorgeous.

Sexy.

Okay, Juliet, that's enough attractive adjectives. You have to stop thinking about how absolutely kissable this man looks and say something.

"Hey, Jules," he says, beating me to it. My name on his lips does something weird to my belly. It flips like he's just said the sexiest thing in the world. Deep and rumbling. I want to bottle it up and make it my ringtone. But that would be weird, super weird, considering he's my best friend's brother. And the last thing I need right now is a boyfriend.

Okay. I need to calm my brain down right now. It's been years since I was attracted to someone that wasn't my ex; that's all this is. Parker is the first attractive guy I've seen in a while, and my body and brain are having a completely normal reaction. But I still need to shut it down.

"Hey," I say, hoping my voice sounds normal. Neither Blair nor Parker looks at me weirdly, so I think I'm good. "Good to see you—it's been what? Five years?"

"Six," he says, the tips of his ears turning pink. "Not that I'm keeping track." He clears his throat. "Should we get checked in or should I just carry all of Blair's luggage for the rest of the day?"

I move into action. "We can check in. Then I've got to go to the Mynt Mingle and Jingle and after that is a VIP meet and greet. I think you two can come to the Mingle and Jingle, but I think you need a ticket for the meet-and-greet."

Blair falls into step behind me, leaving Parker with her bags in the middle of the lobby. I pull my own suit-case behind me. "It's gonna be fine," she says. "I booked us a couples' massage in two days. It wasn't included in your package, and I know we aren't a couple, but I also know you—you'll need something to reset you in the middle of all this."

"Thank you," I say, already feeling a little less appre-hensive about the week. With Blair by my side, I know I can do this.

Chapter 2

Parker

T he resort we're staying at is nice, nicer than any place I've ever visited, but my sister would say that's because I'm a cheapskate. I'm not cheap, I just like to save money, which means I'd never pay for a place like this with my own money. I watch as Blair and Juliet—Jules—make their way to the check-in counter, careful not to watch Juliet's hips as she walks.

I fail miserably. They still sway just like they used to. But she's got more muscle now, in her legs and her shoulders, than she did in high school, and I'm thanking whatever gods of Christmas are up there that she's an athlete who likes to wear leggings and tight sweaters to show off her glorious body. I wonder how soft her hips would be under my hands, or if they'd be firm since she's always playing soccer.

I shouldn't be thinking this. I definitely shouldn't be noticing. Having a crush on my older sister's best friend always made me feel a bit dumb. She's so out of my league and never looked twice at me. I was a geeky, nerdy little brother, and I still am the geeky, nerdy little brother. I'm twenty-four and already have my master's degree in mathematics. I'm currently teaching at UNC in Greeley while pursuing my doctorate in mathematics. I'm a certified nerd, and she's the pretty, cool athlete. In no world would she ever give me a second glance.

But she did. You saw her checking you out earlier. She tried to hide it, but her gaze definitely lingered on you. And her eyes when she saw you? Yup. She's interested. Or at least thinks you're attractive.

I try to ignore the thoughts in my head. I need to ignore them. I cannot feed the dumb, misplaced boyhood crush I had six years ago. I told myself then that I had to get over Juliet Morgan. I tell her that every time I watch one of her games on TV. She's not mine to want, and the fact that she told Blair it was "totally okay" that I came with them on this trip doesn't mean a single thing.

It is precisely why I brought three one-thousand-page fantasy novels to keep me occupied this week. I'll be here, but I can't hang out with Jules. Just seeing her made my heart go wild, and the crush I thought I was over came back in full force. No way will I last a week of hearing her talk and laugh, watching her ogle all the attractive male athletes who are sure to be at this event. I'm a nobody; I do best when I'm invisible or in front of a classroom full of college freshmen. There's no chance she'll ever give me another glance, even if she did check me out.

And even if she did, I don't do flings, which is the only thing we could have since we don't live in the same state and both have careers. I've got to shake this crush; nothing good will come from letting these feelings stew.

"This one is ours," Blair calls out as she takes the two steps up to our cabin door. It doesn't look huge, but maybe it's bigger on the inside? The resort has a huge lodge as its main building, then little cabins sprinkled along the mountainside. We're staying in a cabin instead of the main lodge.

She unlocks the door and Juliet disappears in after her. I take a deep breath of the cold mountain air before following them inside. The cabin is stifling. I look at the heat dial on the wall next to the door—it's turned up to almost eighty, so I turn it down and hear the furnace shut off. In the front room, there's a love seat and a tiny TV over a fireplace and a half-size kitchen with a mini fridge and a microwave. Guess they want everyone to eat at the resort, which makes sense—more ways for them to earn money if the guests have to eat at their restaurants.

Blair disappears down the hall. "There are two rooms, one with a twin bed and one with a queen. You get the twin, Parker."

I haven't slept in a twin bed in years. I'm not exactly a small man, but for this week, being able to shut the door and have some space from Juliet, I can handle it.

"Sounds good," I call back.

"Sorry," Juliet says. "They said the cabin sleeps three, but I didn't realize that one of the beds would be small. I can take the twin."

"Nope." Blair reappears. "I am not sharing a bed with my stinky brother."

"Ha ha," I say, not laughing. At least I'm not actually

trying to impress Juliet, because Blair would be ruining that for me. She's ruined it with every single girl I've tried to date over the years. Or maybe it's just me; I haven't figured that out yet. But Blair likes to meddle. "I'll have you know I haven't been your stinky brother since elementary school and didn't know what deodorant was."

"Some things linger in the brain forever." Blair shudders. "And I do not want to sleep next to you."

"It's fine," I say, moving my suitcase past her. "I'll take the room with the single bed." Makes everything less awkward that way. It'll be a room I can retreat to when I need a minute to myself, which I'm sure I'll have plenty of, since Blair has talked nonstop about all of the events that Juliet has to be part of, so I can just enjoy the holiday in the cabin. Away from everyone. Peaceful and quiet, just the way I like it.

"Hurry, though," Blair calls out from the room with the queen bed. "We've got to get to the welcome thing that Jules needs to be at."

I hear a muffled groan. "Why did I let my manager talk me into this? I'm not meant for all this socializing."

"It's for the children!" Blair calls out in a sing-songy voice, making Juliet laugh. Gosh, I love the sound of her laugh. In high school, when she was at our house, I lived for the moments I could get her to laugh. Unfortunately for me, the crush raging in my heart wants to make her laugh again. This is not good.

"Do you think I should change into some of the Mynt apparel I got?" she asks.

"Do it," Blair says, and that's when I realize I'm still standing in the doorway of my room, just listening to them talk like some sort of creep. I step into my small room. There's a small dresser on one side of the room and a twin bed on the other. I could unpack my stuff, but I'm not sure if it's worth it. I'd rather live out of my suitcase. It's just easier that way—I know where everything is and won't have to remember which drawers I put everything in.

I grab the first novel in the new trilogy I hope to read this week and plop down on the very stiff bed. Maybe I'll sleep on that tiny couch out in the main room; it could be more comfortable than this. I've read the first page when there's a knock on the doorframe. I look up, expecting my sister, but it's Juliet, in a bright green hoodie that has a peppermint above her chest. Not that I'm looking at her chest. Just her hoodie. Which makes her green eyes seem to pop more than usual. I swear I could get lost looking into her eyes, not that I'd ever have the chance to look at her for that long.

"You coming?" she asks, breaking up my thoughts.

I wasn't planning on it, but if she's asking? Then yeah, I'm coming. "Yup."

Chapter 3

Juliet

Someone is already speaking into a microphone when I pull open the door for the Mynt Mingle and Jingle. We're late, and a man—who kind of looks like Santa would if he wore a red suit covered in peppermints instead of his classic red suit—is talking animatedly into the microphone all about how this week is about *giving* instead of selling. This must be Mr. Mynt, the guy in charge of this whole event, clothing brand, and the resort. While I do find Christmas pretty magical, he seems a bit over the top.

"There are two seats over there," Blair whispers, pointing to our right. "We'll go sit over there. You should go see if you can sit by those people; they look like they might be athletes."

The group she points toward is sitting near the back, which is fine by me. Even if I'd rather hang out with Blair and Parker. As I approach the seats, Mr. Mynt says something about an icebreaker and gives instructions. People stand, and I'm moved into a small circle where we all sit on the chairs that people have been moving around.

There's chatter throughout the room, and I glance around, trying to see where Parker and Blair ended up, but they're lost in the mass of athletes. I don't actually know if they were supposed to come to this with me since it might only be for the athletes, but I doubt Blair will care. When I turn back to my group, a girl with dark hair is finishing answering the question. "...would be Prancer because everyone loves watching me on the green, and I always give a good show, bringing more viewers to the game of golf."

I swivel in my seat so I can see what the question actually is up on a screen at the front of the room. *If I were one of Santa's reindeer, who would I be and why?* What kind of question is that? I wonder what Parker's answer would be. I shouldn't wonder that at all. Just because he grew up and is all hot now doesn't mean I need to get close to him; in fact, I should do the opposite and stay as far away from him as I can. Okay, the question. I don't even know the names of the reindeer. How am I supposed to answer this question?

Another girl answers while I discreetly pull out my phone and search "names of Santa's reindeer." Then it's my turn. "Hi everyone," I say with more energy than I feel. This may be silly, but I'll be spending the week with some of these people; I may as well get to know them. Plus, if I focus on them, I'll have less time to think about Parker's glasses. "I'm Juliet Morgan and I play soccer in DC and for the U.S. women's team. And I guess if I had to pick a reindeer, I'd pick Rudolph, if that counts, because when I get cold, my nose turns bright red."

Our small group of five chuckles at this.

Chloe, an ice skater, goes next, then a hockey player named Holden goes last, talking about how fast he is on the ice. We should race—I wonder if he's as fast on the field as he is on the ice. I don't like hockey players much; they're too grumpy and all that, and this one seems like all the others I've met. Should I mention that my one and only ex was a soccer player, and that might be why I don't have a favorable opinion about male athletes at the moment? Thankfully, we're all saved from making awkward small talk as "Jingle Bells" plays over the loud-speakers and Mr. Mynt returns to the stage. "We've got just enough time for a group photo before our VIP meet-and-greet. If you're not an athlete, we'll have you exit the south door."

After a lot of shuffling and several phone cameras pointed in our direction, we're ushered to our different tables to meet the fans who got the VIP tickets. I wish Blair were here; there's a good chance she read the welcome packet more thoroughly than I did and would have a better idea of who received these tickets. Did people have to buy them? Did they win them?

I'll never know because the doors open and people come flooding in. They're buzzing around to various tables, and pretty soon I'm signing photos with my face on them and my jersey that people brought, and taking pictures with fans. Time simply flies by.

By the end of the meet-and-greet, my brain is fried. I do better on the field. I do better with my team. I love meeting fans; it's one of the fun parts of my job, but it's also exhausting when I'm the one who has to do all the talking. Usually, at things like this, my team is also here, and I don't have to do all the talking and smiling.

Today, though, it was all me. I mean, there are a ton of other athletes here, and their tables all looked as busy as mine, but I'm drained.

I pull out my phone to text Blair.

ME

> Where are you? I could use a massage
> right about now. Or food, I'm starving.

She texts back almost immediately.

BLAIR

> We're just hanging out in the lobby. You
> should come smile at Parker or bring
> him an athlete who will make him stop
> being so grumpy. We can eat at one of
> the restaurants at the resort or one in
> town.

The thought of introducing a different athlete to Parker makes me frown. But why shouldn't I? He's not mine to claim. And if I think he's attractive, I'm sure other people will too. But right now, I'm not in the mood to talk to more strangers, so I slip out of the big ballroom and into the lobby, scanning the very decorated space for my friends. I find them sitting on one of the large sofas that sit around a Christmas tree. They haven't seen me yet, so I give myself exactly ten seconds to admire Parker

17

and all of his gorgeousness. Men should not be allowed to wear glasses, because their glasses are doing such weird things to my brain.

He glances up and our eyes meet. His small smile grows into a wide smirk before he lifts a hand to wave me over. I've been caught. There's no way around it now.

I know that he knows that I was totally staring at him.

Blair, thankfully, is looking down at her phone, oblivious to me ogling her brother, which I *should not* be doing. Ten seconds was too much and not enough all at the same time. I have got to get a grip. Maybe I actually should introduce Parker to one of the girls I met today. Being jealous would be better than getting caught staring.

Chapter 4

Parker

She was staring at me. Utterly and completely staring at me. It was like I could feel someone watching me, and when I looked up, there was Juliet, eyes drinking me in. There's no way she can deny it. Not with how her cheeks turned pink and she looked away as soon as my eyes met hers.

Nope. She was staring at me, which is absolutely the worst news for my poor teenage crush that I can't even call a teenage crush now since I'm an adult and this is a full-blown adult crush.

And she was staring at me. It means—I think—she likes what she sees.

"What are you so smug about?" Blair asks me without looking up from her phone. For the past two hours of the VIP meet-and-greet, she's been locked in on her phone, saying she was managing some work stuff. It's ironic, since she's the one who told me I *had* to come with her this week to get away from work. But she can't seem to look away.

"How do you know I'm smug?" I ask.

"I can feel it oozing off of you."

"Whatever," I grunt. "Not smug." Okay, so I'm a little bit smug. My older sister's best friend was staring at me.

A person—okay, I know it's Jules, but maybe referring to her simply as a person will help keep my feelings at bay—approaches us. "I'm starving," she says. I jump up with a little too much enthusiasm and Blair eyes me suspiciously.

"What?" I ask, trying to play it off. "I haven't eaten anything since breakfast. Let's go find some lunch."

Lunch turns out to be overpriced sandwiches at one of the resort's restaurants. The sandwiches aren't bad, but they are not worth the fifteen dollars each we had to pay for them.

The sky is overcast as we make our way back to the cabin.

"Later tonight, we can go to the hot chocolate bar," Blair says. "At least all of the activities the resort offers are free. Too bad their food is pricey."

"I can cover you two if you want me to," Jules says. "I mean, it's my fault that you're here since I practically dragged you. I wouldn't be a very good host if I didn't pay for things like food."

Blair links her arm through one of Jules's. I wish it were me, but that would be weird, so I stuff my hands into my pockets. "Nope. Not gonna happen. I make good money as a lawyer, and Parker is bringing in the big bucks as a university professor."

I cough out a laugh. "Pretty sure I'm not making the big bucks. But I'm good," I add when I see concern flit

20

across Juliet's face. "I can cover my own very expensive meals for six days."

"I can pay for you two," Jules says again.

"Let's go chill in the cabin for a bit," Blair says, changing the subject. "You look like you could use some quiet time."

"Quiet time" ends up being the two of them playing card games with the cards Blair brought in the main room, while I settle onto my somewhat uncomfortable twin bed and try to start my first book.

But Juliet's laugh seems to fill the cabin as she and Blair catch up, and I'm thrown back to high school when they'd be laughing while they did homework in the room next to mine. It's always been hard for me to focus when Juliet is around.

Around four in the afternoon, I'm just about to head out and ask if anyone wants to go explore since I'm getting stir crazy, when Juliet appears in my doorway.

"I don't know if you've heard, but the sounds coming from the bathroom are not good," she says with a grimace.

I haven't heard anything, simply because I've been hyper-focused on trying to read my book, though I've only made it through one chapter in several hours. It's not working.

"Oh?"

The sound of my sister throwing up enters the space from across the hall. "Oh."

Juliet nods. "I don't know if it's food poisoning or a virus or something. One second she was fine, and the next she was greenish and ran to the bathroom."

I frown. Neither option is good. I had the same sandwich that Blair got at lunch, and I feel fine. But if it's a virus...

"I think we should go stock up on some microwavable soup, crackers, and anything else that helps with nausea," Juliet says, putting a finger up with each item she mentions. "And maybe some vitamin C so we don't catch whatever she has."

"I noticed a little grocery store a few minutes away, more into town, if you want to go now?" I ask, easing off the bed. I set my book on top of the dresser.

Another sound of retching hits our ears, and Juliet pales. "I think now would be good. I hate the sound of throwing up."

I nod. "Let's go then."

We grab our jackets, and I tell Blair through the closed bathroom door where we're headed. She offers a weak groan in reply and then we're off.

My body hums with nervous energy as Juliet climbs into the passenger seat of my car. What I wouldn't give to call my high school buddy, Max, right now and tell him that Juliet Morgan is in my car. She's silent for the first few minutes as I hum along to the holiday music playing on the radio.

"If she really does have a virus, I can't stay in that cabin all day," she says, breaking the silence.

Before I can think better of it, I find myself suggesting, "We can do all the activities the resort has to offer. There are a bunch, aren't there? We can get the list and try to do them all."

Her eyes widen, clearly surprised at my idea. "You'd do that with me? I mean, I know I don't want to be in the cabin if she's sick, but I know you might not want to be around all those people. I might not want to be around all those people."

I'd walk to the moon for her if she asked, but I don't say that. "Sure, why not? I couldn't focus on reading with the two of you laughing and giggling anyway. It'll be fun. A different kind of adventure." Do I want to spend my holiday vacation around a ton of people? Not particularly. Will I do it so I can spend time around Jules? Absolutely.

"Sorry, I didn't realize we were being so loud."

"The cabin walls, despite seeming to be made out of wood, aren't very soundproof, and my door was open."

"But you don't mind doing things?"

"Nah, it'll be fun." Plus, it means I get to spend time with her, which is more than I could have hoped for or dreamt of. While we've spent a lot of time together over the years, it's never been one-on-one—Blair is always with us. This will be the first time that Jules and I do something just the two of us. And I'd be lying if I said that didn't thrill me.

Chapter 5

Juliet

I've got the resort itinerary pulled up on my phone as we walk around the small store, putting things like microwavable soup and crackers into the little cart that Parker is pushing around.

"We should do the sleigh ride. I've always wanted to ride one of those," I say, realizing only after the words are out of my mouth that a sleigh ride at Christmastime is one of those things couples do in romance movies.

"That'd be great," Parker says, grabbing some anti-nausea medicine off the shelf. I have to hold back a full-body shiver. Maybe he doesn't think it's romantic, or maybe he just doesn't care. "And didn't Blair say she booked a massage for the two of you? If you don't mind, we could do that too. I've got a killer knot in my neck, and a massage that my sister paid for? Sign me up."

I shift to look at him as he scans the different medications on the shelf. He doesn't seem to be feeling the same way I do. I don't seem to be affecting him the way he's affecting me. I shake away the feeling. "Sure. Massages are always great."

By the time we're in the checkout line, I've got a tidy little list on the notes app of my phone of all the things we're going to do. And since Parker will never see the list, at the very bottom, I have my very own item to cross off at the end of this week.

- Don't fall for Parker James

It'll be great. What could possibly go wrong with this plan?

Back at the cabin, Blair thanks us for everything we bought before rushing back to the bathroom. We take that as our cue to explore the resort and maybe grab some hot chocolate if we can find the hot chocolate bar Blair mentioned earlier.

"So, how's soccer?" Parker asks at the same time as I blurt out, "Do you like being a math professor?"

He chuckles, a deep laugh that makes my belly swirl with attraction. I try to shove it down, but I don't know how much more shoving I can do at this point.

"Being a professor is good. I like it. I do think I want to go back into the secondary schools, though, and teach high school or middle school. College is good, but I feel like I could have more of an impact teaching high school."

"That would be so cool." I stuff my hands in the

pockets of my coat to keep me from reaching toward Parker and linking my arm with his, like Blair did earlier with me. "I've thought about coaching at a high school or a club team when I retire."

His hazel eyes swing to meet mine. "You'd be great at that."

I shrug off his compliment. "I briefly helped at a summer camp a few years back. It was just a few days, but I think I loved it almost as much as I love playing the game."

"You should do it then." We've reached the main lodge and Parker grabs the door handle, pulling it open and holding it for me. Swoon.

Gosh, I really should have gone on that date my teammate tried to set me up on a couple of weeks ago. Maybe then everything Parker is doing wouldn't feel so perfect. So romantic. It's a door, nothing more. We both have to go through it.

"We'll see. I want to play for as long as I can. I've got at least a few more really good years." Training as hard as I do, playing the way I do, isn't exactly easy on my body. I'm only twenty-eight and I'm already feeling the fact that I've played soccer for twenty-three years. In my mind right now, I imagine that I'll either play as long as I can while also having kids, or I'll retire once I hit thirty-five so that I can settle down and still have time to have a family. I want kids, the picket fence, a husband coming home from work each night, and a night with us laughing, flirting, and just being in love. It feels idyllic—it probably is, but it's still the dream. Well, the dream once my first dream—soccer, preferably on an Olympic team—ends. But I don't like to think about closing this chapter of my life. As much as I daydream about a future that has a husband, kids, and maybe a pet or two, I'm not finished playing the game I love the most.

Chapter 6

Parker

"I'm stealing your bed," Blair grumbles from the couch the next morning. Last night she said she would sleep on the couch so she wouldn't get me or Juliet sick, but she looks even worse today. "That couch is made of rocks."

I can't help it as a laugh escapes. "Pretty sure it's not."

"I'm stealing your bed and you can try to sleep on the couch if you don't believe me," she says, pulling a blanket she found in the linen closet tightly around her. "You have basically five minutes to get your stuff out so I can lie down and go to sleep before I barf again."

"Noted," I say.

I don't know where I'll sleep tonight or where to put my bag, but I know better than to get in Blair's way. She gets what she wants, and when she's sick? She definitely gets everything she wants. I'm not about to stand in her way.

Thankfully, all my stuff is still in my bag. I grab my glasses off of the dresser, slide them on, and head back to the small living area. Blair, wrapped in her blanket, shuffles down the hallway and into the room I just vacated. The door shuts softly behind her. I sit on the couch, grimacing when I realize she might be right: there is absolutely no give. It's as solid as a rock.

Just my luck.

The door at the end of the hallway opens, and Juliet walks down the hallway, gathering her hair into a messy bun. She stops short when she sees me on the couch.

"Blair took my bed," I inform her. "She didn't get much sleep last night."

She plops onto the couch next to me, closing her eyes. "I didn't either. I think I woke up every single time she threw up."

"That's brutal."

She murmurs an agreement. "Thankfully, we have a massage scheduled in an hour. Should we get breakfast and then go to the spa?"

"I don't have to go if it'll be weird," I say.

Her eyes snap open, narrowing on me. "I should have known you'd back out right at the first thing."

"Whoa, no. No way am I backing out."

"Then you get to have a massage too."

The idea of a stranger rubbing their hands all over my neck, back, and shoulders makes me want to crawl out of my skin, even though I do have a knot in my neck. I'll get through it for Jules. I said I'd do all the activities with her, and if she wants to do this, then I'll do it.

"I might work on lesson plans after, though," I say. Yes, it's an excuse, but in all reality, I'm feeling a bit twitchy not working right now. Most of my colleagues love having breaks, but not having classes to teach or a thesis to work on—which I could, but I didn't bring anything for that since I thought Blair would kill me—makes me feel like I'm going to die. I like being busy. Busy is good. Busy means my thoughts aren't running a mile a minute.

I hate when I'm quiet around strangers, I always feel so awkward. But I also don't want to be the one who says anything. So a massage? Definitely not my thing. But for Jules? I'll do it. For her, I can get over the feeling of wanting to crawl out of my skin. I don't know why. It's completely ridiculous since she doesn't like me that way and I shouldn't like her in any way. She's my sister's best friend, but something about her seems to slow my mind down—not like anything is wrong, but in a way that makes me feel calm.

All the confidence I had yesterday when I proposed the idea to do everything melts away. Maybe I should have thought about this more before I spoke. Too late now, though.

Snapping fingers appear in front of my eyes. "Earth to Parker."

Mentally, I shake myself. "Sorry." This has been happening a lot, me getting so caught up in my thoughts that I don't realize things are happening around me. But I'm with Jules; it shouldn't have happened with her.

"It's all good. Just as long as you promise to do everything with me, you can still plan your lessons or whatever."

"I'm all in," I say, holding out my hand. "We can shake on it."

Her hand slides into mine, her fingers wrapping around my hand as she squeezes, and warmth slides up my arm as she shakes once. For a beat, neither of us pulls their hand away. I let go after a second, though, because as much as I want to keep her hand in mine, I don't want to make it weird.

"Good, should we go? We've got a busy day ahead of us." She grabs her coat from the hook by the door. "I was looking at everything the resort offers regularly, along with all the activities they're hosting for the charity event. We could have even joined in on a ballroom competition —like *Dancing with the Stars*—but they started rehearsal for that a couple of weeks ago." She shrugs like this is no big deal. "I guess I should have read all the info my manager sent me before last night. I could have signed up for the dancing competition. But I wasn't really planning on doing most of the activities until yesterday. But I think it will be fun."

My gut clenches. She changed her plans for me, and she doesn't seem mad about it. I'm not sure what to think about that, so I don't.

"Well, I'm not much of a dancer," I say, keeping it light. How she lives her life—all carefree and not reading details; I guess that's why she has a manager, someone who can do some of that stuff for her—shouldn't impact me. Not everyone has to be as meticulous as I am. Most people aren't, and that's okay.

She grins up at me. "Well, we do get to do a polar plunge instead."

"Uh, what?" If she's talking about what I think she's talking about...

"You know, when you wear a swimsuit or your underwear and jump into freezing cold water for a few seconds? That's the main charity event that I'm supposed to be at. All the others are optional, but that one? I have to be there, which means you do too. I think all the athletes were assigned different events that they have to be at, and that one is mine."

My stomach twists. I'm not a huge fan of water in general, but freezing water? This woman has got to be out of her mind if she thinks I'll get in the frozen pond with her.

"I practically hear your wheels turning, trying to figure a way to get out of it," she says as we step into the frosty morning air. "But you can't. Also, there will be dancing. There's a big ball on Christmas Eve."

"I'll go only if you dance with me." The words tumble out, but the boy with the teenage crush inside of me is growing stronger and stronger, and if I get a chance to dance with Juliet, hold her close in my arms? I'm not going to let that pass.

She gives me a smirk. "Only if you do the polar plunge."

"You're the worst, you know that, right?"

She tosses her head back as she laughs. "But you love me."

I swallow. She's only joking, but would she have said that if she knew what my feelings actually are? That, as hard as I've tried to forget about her and move on from my boyhood crush, I can't? I'm drawn to her, possibly a little bit in love with her. It's only going to make the end of this week hurt that much more, because my heart will be broken, and it will be my own fault.

Chapter 7

Juliet

First up this morning is our spa appointment. I tried to convince Blair to cancel it last night. Getting a couples massage with Parker? We aren't a couple, and no way was I about to strip down to my underwear and have only a thin sheet covering me while he was getting a massage on the table next to me. No thank you.

But she wasn't having it. So now the two of us are heading to the resort's spa and I'm thinking of all the ways that this could end badly or awkwardly. Mostly I'm worried about the fact that I'll be naked under a sheet only a few feet away from Parker who will also be naked. Under his own sheet. But sure, this is a great idea.

Maybe if I'd told her that I'm attracted to him, she would have let me cancel. But I can't tell my best friend that I think her brother is hot. She'd make fun of me until we were ninety.

We head to the spa in agonizing silence. I'd love to say something, but all I can think about is the past few massages I've gotten and the fact that in less than ten minutes, I'll probably be extremely uncomfortable under a blanket.

"Maybe we shouldn't do this," I say, stopping short in front of the spa entrance.

Parker gives me a sly grin. "You're gonna be the one backing out on me? That, I didn't see coming."

I shift from one foot to the other. "It's a couples massage."

"So?"

"We aren't a couple," I state the obvious.

His grin only widens. "So? Would it make you more comfortable if we pretended to be one? Or would that make this entire thing more awkward."

Okay, so maybe he thinks this is awkward too. Not just me. "That'd definitely be weird."

"We could tell them we're siblings."

I scrunch my face. I don't have a brother, but I'm pretty sure you don't think about how attractive your sibling is at the sight of them in glasses. "No."

"Alright." He stuffs his hands in his pockets. "Well, I personally hate the idea of a stranger touching me, and as much as Blair assured me that 'I would love it,' I'm happy to go find something else to do."

Tension leaves my body. "We should go find something else to do. We could go find the hot chocolate or something."

"Love this plan," he says. "I'll go in and cancel the appointment."

He heads into the spa to cancel our appointment. And as much as I regret missing the chance to see Parker shirtless, I know we'll have a better time if we skip this activity. A few minutes later, he returns. "We're good to go. Should we go find that hot chocolate bar? I think you mentioned it yesterday, or maybe it was Blair. I don't remember now."

"Yes." We had a light breakfast of toast at the cabin, but hot chocolate sounds like the perfect holiday treat.

We find the hot chocolate. I add a candy cane to mine and Parker doesn't add anything extra to his.

"I'm a hot chocolate purist," he says, taking a sip.

"I have to add a little peppermint." I sigh as I take a sip of the minty and chocolatey liquid. "This was a much better idea."

"What? You didn't like the idea of the two of us lying on tables super close to each other while strangers rub us down with oils that are probably supposed to make us feel romantic things," he says with a straight face.

"Um, not particularly?"

He bumps my shoulder with his. "I'm teasing. It would have been weird. I don't know what Blair was thinking."

"I think she was thinking she wanted a massage and then she got sick and wanted us to do it."

"She likes to gift things that she likes." He chuckles. "It isn't usually a problem. The two of you would have had a great time."

I shrug. "Maybe. I prefer ice baths to massages."

"I guess you'll love the polar plunge then."

"Well, I usually take an ice bath in the training room, which isn't freezing outside, so this will be different."

"Probably not that different."

"I'm not going to be sore though. It'll just be my regular self dunking my body into a freezing cold lake."

He takes a sip of hot chocolate. "You're really not making me look forward to that activity."

I hold back a grimace. "I'm not all that thrilled either."

"But hey, here's to new adventures. Even if they're terrifying."

I look at him curiously, wondering if he's terrified of going into the frozen lake or if something else scares him.

We hang around our cabin until it's afternoon and time for the cookie decorating activity. I scroll through my phone, reading the instructions about this activity and where it is. "It says that the cookie decorating is in the fireside lounge, but I don't know where that is."

Parker, who hasn't said much since we left the cabin, turns to me. "I'm sure there's a map of the place somewhere, or we can ask someone."

"Look at you, problem solving," I say, but really, I'm just thankful that he seems to have his wits about him. I need to get into the fireside lounge and start decorating cookies so I can stop feeling so weird about the fact that I'll be spending all week with Parker.

"That is basically what I do for a living, solve problems. Though, they're usually math problems." He gives me a charming smile that has my stomach doing flips. I really should shut this down; what he said wasn't even flirting, but...what would be the harm in a little flirting this week? It's not like Blair will notice. And it's obvious with how he's been smirking at me that it wouldn't be difficult to flirt. Right? I've only ever dated one guy, and it wasn't exactly a healthy relationship. But I feel so inexperienced. It's not like I'm old—I'm not even thirty yet—but I haven't really flirted with anyone in years, I'm a little rusty.

"I love a man who can solve problems," I say, my voice cracking at the end like it decided my terrible attempt at flirting was truly terrible and had to save me from myself.

Parker stumbles on the completely clear path; the tips of his ears are pink, which is cute. He doesn't respond, though, which wasn't the reaction I was hoping for. But I surprised him, I think. So that's something.

The lodge is warm and smells like cinnamon when we step into the lobby. There's a sign to our right pointing to the ballroom that says "rehearsal," but there are no other signs anywhere for any of the other events.

"Let's ask over there." Parker points to an information desk, off to the side of the check-in counter. There are people dressed in Mr. Mynt's athletic gear everywhere around us, so you'd think we could find where we need to go on our own.

The man sitting at the information desk doesn't look up when we approach. Parker clears his throat. "Could you help us find out where—"

The man cuts him off by holding up a finger before going back to typing furiously on his computer. Parker looks at me and I just raise my eyebrows and shrug. Whenever I travel with the team, our manager takes care of things like this while the rest of us hang out until we're told where to go. I'm not used to figuring things out for myself, which now, as I'm standing here, feels incredibly silly. I'm twenty-eight. I should know how to find out where to go without leaning on an adultier adult to do that for me, even if that is her job.

Parker plays with the little business card on the counter. It's green with little peppermints all around the edges. Finally, the man looks up at us. "Can I help you?" he clips.

"Uh, yeah," I say. "We're looking for the cookie-decorating activity."

"That's for athletes and their guests," he says snootily.

"Well, she's an athlete," Parker jumps in. "And I'm her guest."

The man eyes us warily, like he can't believe someone is asking him for information, at the information desk.

"I'm going to need your name." He looks back at his computer, fingers poised, ready to type.

"Juliet Morgan," I say.

He types, then scrolls and clicks on something.

"This is her," Parker says, holding out his phone. I catch a glimpse of my sports profile on the U.S. team's website. "She's a pro."

"Mm-hm," the man murmurs. "The two of you can head to the fireside lounge."

"Which is where?" I ask, grinding my teeth together. Can this guy just give us directions so we can be on our way to all of the Christmas things? Why does he work at such a festive resort if he's so grouchy?

"Down the hall, you'll find stairs, and you can take them to the third floor. The fireside lounge is down the hall and to the left once you get up there." His mouth turns to a thin line before he sighs. "Can I help you with anything else?"

"Nope, we're all set, thanks." Parker grabs my hand and tugs me away from the information desk. Just like earlier, when we shook hands, it feels like flames move up my entire body which is funny because there's a spread of goosebumps that I'm grateful are now covered by my coat and sweater. Why do his hands have to feel so perfect?

There's movement across the lobby, and my stomach drops as my eyes connect with my exes. I cling to Parker's hand as I see Axel moving toward us. The good feeling I had only a second ago flees my body as I see the last person I expected to see here. The guy who broke my heart. No, that's an understatement of the century. Axel completely destroyed me, and seeing him sends me back to six months ago, when I couldn't even get out of bed after the last time I saw him.

"Juliet?" He breaks out into a wide grin when he reaches me, and my stomach rolls with nausea.

"Hey, Axel," I manage to say. Beside him is one of his teammates on the U.S. men's soccer team. "I didn't know you'd be here."

"It was kind of a last-minute thing." He glances at Parker, whose hand I'm still clinging to. "Who are you?"

Parker's eyebrows rise almost to his hairline. I squeeze his hand tighter, wishing I could just walk away. "Who are you?" Parker repeats the question back to Axel.

Axel narrows his eyes at him. "I've been dating Juliet off and on for two years. But we're on a break. I didn't realize she was seeing other people."

I clench my jaw because *nothing* that just came out of his mouth is anywhere close to the truth. But I can't seem to make my tongue move to call him out. I hate that he's always made me feel so small. My eyes flick to Parker who's watching me carefully. His eyebrows lift slightly and I bite my lip, unsure of what to say. Mostly, I just want Axel to go away.

"Well, I guess you're really the ex now, huh?" Parker stands a tiny bit taller, his huge hand engulfing mine even more. "'Cause we've been dating for a few months."

I see fury burn in Axel's eyes. His friend and teammate steps between him and Parker. "It's not worth it, man."

Axel looks at me. "You're right, it's not. Because when this ends in a week, she'll come back to me, just like she always does. We're meant to be." Without another glance at Parker, he walks away.

"You okay?" Parker asks, leading me to a couch. "You're shaking."

I hate Axel. I hate him. Maybe that's a terrible thing to say, considering I don't hate anything, but I do. I hate him. The nerve he has, trying to get under my skin in front of Parker. Parker.

I look at him. "I am so sorry. I couldn't seem to let go of your hand after I saw him. I wasn't trying to do anything..."

He searches my face. "Are you okay?"

No, not really. I hate how much seeing my ex shakes

41

me up. I avoid tabloids and news, and he's blocked on all of my socials, but seeing him here? I wasn't ready for that.

"I'm fine." I push down the worry building in my chest. The last time I ran into Axel was six months ago, right after I got the news that I wouldn't be going to the Olympics due to my injury and he was about to leave. We spent the week together, and it felt so good, so normal, so right. I thought that maybe it was for real that time. I was completely in love with him, even after all of our on-again, off-again relationship.

Then he left for the Olympics. I thought we had an understanding of what we were—together—and maybe this time we'd make it work. Instead, he ghosted me and was posting pictures with his "new girlfriend" the very next week. Some model who he'd flown out to support him while his team played in the Olympics.

I was crushed.

Blair flew out to see me in DC when she hadn't heard from me in a week. She found me curled under a blanket on the couch, re-watching *Grey's Anatomy*. She got me out of my depressive episode and helped me get back on my meds and back on track with training so that the next time the Olympics come around, I'll be ready to go. I don't think I'd be here without her.

"You don't seem fine." Parker's voice shakes me out of my memory. My hands shake slightly and he grabs one, threading his fingers through mine. "Look at me," he says, his voice low and calm. "Breathe when I do, in...out...in... out...there you go."

"I'm sorry," I whisper. I hate that I feel this way.

Memories of that week after he left, when I found out he was with someone else, are hitting me full force. I want to go hide under a blanket. But I won't, because that would be letting him win, and I'm not going to let that happen again.

"Do you want to talk about what just happened?"

I shake my head. "I'd really like to go decorate some cookies if that's all right with you."

"Sure thing."

I'm thankful he doesn't push. I should probably tell him why I just freaked out when one of the most famous soccer players in the world just claimed I'd come running back to him, but I don't. Instead, we find the stairs and make our way to the third floor.

Outside of the fireside lounge, I tense, hearing the familiar laughter of my ex.

"We don't have to go in there," Parker offers.

"No, I want to." I square my shoulders. I can do this.

He slips his hand into mine. "I don't mind playing your boyfriend this week, at least when he's around, if that would make you feel better. And if that doesn't make you feel better, you can completely forget that dumb suggestion, and we can go make cookies and I'll be your best friend's little brother and nothing more."

My heart melts. "That's really sweet of you to offer."

Parker pulls his hand from mine, a flash of hurt in his eyes. I didn't mean to hurt him.

"Best friend's little brother, got it." I want to tell him that his offer isn't just sweet, it's perfect. Too perfect, even. He shouldn't give me that kindness, and maybe he wouldn't if he knew what type of person I've been. If

43

Parker knew that I flung myself at Axel over and over and over, and that it took him sending me into a depressive episode to realize that I wasn't ever going to be good enough for him. I'm Axel's backup plan, and I hate that. But I also can't accept Parker's offer.

I don't get a chance to say any of that, though, because Parker steps into the room and I have no choice but to follow him. A woman beams at us from a table to our right. "Are you an athlete checking in?"

"I'm not," Parker says, then points to me. "But she is."

I tell her my name and she looks through a list—I guess they're keeping track of who goes where. I can't really focus though; instead I scan the room, and sure enough, I see Axel sitting at a table with a family with two young kids, probably members of the Winterbrook community. My stomach flips, threatening to lose my lunch as I watch as the parents laugh at something he says. My breathing comes in quick gasps, like I can't breathe in deeply.

"We'll sit over there," Parker says, gently grabbing my hand and pulling me to the opposite side of the room, where there's an empty table. My breathing is still shallow; I can't focus on anything. "Look at me."

My eyes spring to his honey-brown ones. Which now that I'm looking into them, they seem more golden than brown. I was so distracted by his glasses yesterday that I didn't notice the color of his eyes. I've never noticed the color of his eyes until this moment, I always just assumed they were dark brown like Blair's.

"I want you to look around and tell me five things you can see."

Uh, that's weird, but okay. I avoid looking in Axel's direction again, instead looking at the table in front of me. "Red tablecloth, green and red frosting, sugar cookies that look like Christmas trees, and sprinkles. Was that five?"

He shakes his head. "One more."

"You."

"Good. Now I want you to tell me four things you can hear."

I've never heard of this weird game he's playing, but it's slightly distracting me from Axel, so I go along with it. My breathing slows as I glance around the room, focusing on the noises I'm hearing. "They're playing "Santa Claus is Coming to Town" on a speaker, a girl over there is giggling, another kid is singing "Jingle Bells," and I can hear my voice. What is this game?"

"It's not a game, and I'll explain when we finish. Tell me three things you can touch. Describe the texture or how it feels under your fingers."

I want him to explain now, but when I open my mouth to say as much, he shakes his head. "Three things, Jules."

I sigh. I reach out and touch the plastic tablecloth. "This feels like cheap plastic."

He nods. "What else?"

I touch the faux-fur trim on the end of my sleeve. "This is soft." I reach out and touch his cardigan, because I've been wanting to see if it's as soft as it looks. "This feels...soft and comfortable. Like something I'd want to curl up in while watching a Christmas movie."

"Good," he says. Still staring at my face and not at my hand, which is still stroking his sweater. I know that's weird, but I can't seem to pull my hand away. "Now two things you can smell and one thing you can taste."

"Sugar cookies." I grin. The entire room smells absolutely delightful, like those sugary candles I always used to burn in my bedroom because Mom didn't want them anywhere else in the house. "And I smell cinnamon, I think. Or some other spice."

I look around. I don't actually taste anything right now. I grab a knife from the frosting bowl in front of me and lick it clean. "This is a little bit sweeter than I usually like, but it's good."

"We're gonna need a new knife."

This makes me laugh. "I'm not going to stick this back in the bowl. We have to share that, and who knows where the cookies are going after we decorate them? I don't want to spread all my germs, especially not if I'm carrying whatever Blair has." I shudder, placing the plastic knife on the table. "Now are you going to explain your game or not?"

"It's an anxiety trick," he says, his eyes shifting to the floor as if this is somehow embarrassing.

"Anxiety? I'm not anxious though."

His eyes flit up to mine. "You were completely tense, your shoulders practically up to your ears, and I swear you stopped breathing for a minute. I had to get you to stop thinking about..." He trails off and my heart clenches again. I'd forgotten about Axel for a moment. He continues, "It's a trick I learned when I went to the free therapy my campus offers a couple of years ago."

"You go to therapy?"

He shakes his head. "Well, sometimes. My anxiety isn't bad all the time."

"I didn't know you had anxiety." Blair never said anything.

"I was in denial about it for a while. Didn't think I really had it, but then someone pointed out that I'm always burying myself in schoolwork so that I'm constantly busy. When I told them it was because I didn't want to listen to all the ways I overthink everything else, they said I might have anxiety and that I should talk to a therapist. She gave me some tools, like what I just showed you. It helps ground yourself in the present moment; you're busy focused on your physical surroundings and all of your senses, so your brain has to stop worrying about whatever it was you were worrying about."

I sit there for a moment. Maybe I don't have super intense anxiety, but I did feel like I couldn't breathe since I found out Axel was here. And Parker's trick did help.

"Thanks," I say. "It helped."

He grabs a cookie and a new knife. "Anytime. Now, should we make the best decorated Christmas cookies the world has ever seen?"

A laugh bubbles out of me as I reach for one shaped like a Santa hat. "Sounds like a good plan."

Chapter 8

Parker

Hearing her laughter after seeing her so tense feels like a win, but I'm still concerned. Obviously that jerk did a real number on Juliet. I recognize his face, but I can't think of his name. I don't want to know his name. I want him to leave and then I want to help Juliet forget that he ever existed. I want her tinkling laugh to fill the air all the time. I want a million things that I shouldn't.

I glance around the room. Her ex is behind us, but now he's facing us. He scowls at me and I face my cookie.

"So," I say, "don't look now, but that guy is staring at us. And by staring, I mean he's shooting daggers with his eyes, and I think he wants to kill me."

Her jaw tenses. "He's not violent, just possessive. And stupid. He wants what he can't have, and then when he gets it, he cheats."

Every word out of her mouth makes me dislike this guy more and more. "What do you want me to do?" I ask.

She worries her lip and stares at the cookie in front of her. "I know before I said that it was sweet of you to offer to pretend to be my boyfriend for the week, and I did mean that..."

My heart pounds so fast I can feel it in my head. I blink to stay focused on her.

"Would you...I mean...gosh, I feel so silly asking you to do something like that. Would it be weird? I mean, I'm Blair's best friend. I don't want to put you in an awkward position."

She's nervous about Blair's reaction to all of this? "I'm pretty sure if we explained, Blair would understand."

She nods, still not looking at me. I reach across the small distance and pull her hand into mine. I cannot think about how much I love the feeling of her soft skin under my hands, because this would all be pretend. But if it helps get her ex off her back, then it'll be worth it. At least, that's what I'm trying to tell my heart.

"I can be the best fake boyfriend you've ever had," I say quietly, just so people at the surrounding tables don't hear.

She laughs. "Thanks. But it feels so silly to have to do that. I don't want him to think he has any power over me. I don't want him to be jealous. I just want him to see that I've moved on. I'm not his backup plan. He can't have me anymore."

"You're already doing that," I assure her. "He doesn't have to know this isn't real, but if it'll help him get the message to leave you alone, then I'm all for it."

"It's probably the only thing that would work since he doesn't seem to care what I say," she grumbles.

I lift her chin so she'll meet my eyes. They've got little gold flecks around her pupils. I could get lost in the colors of her eyes, but I don't. Now is the time to focus. "He's a guy who thinks he can have whatever he wants, even when someone says no. I know the type. We're not going to make him jealous, but make it obvious that you're a person, not a toy that he gets to play around with."

It kills me that that's how he's used her in the past. She didn't exactly say that, but I can guess. I've watched too many of the men I work with do the same thing with undergrad students. They treat women—and people in general—as if they're supposed to bow down to their will, that even if they cause any hurt or pain, people will still do their bidding or come running back to them. Juliet deserves more than that.

She blinks back tears. "Why would you do that for me? Help me with this?"

I sigh, pulling my hand from her face and placing it on top of the hand that's holding hers. "You're my sister's best friend." I hope I sound as casual as I can, and that she'll buy it. That she will think the only reason I'm doing this is because of Blair. "She'd kill me if she found out I could have done something and didn't." It may or may not be true, but I'm going with it.

"You're a good man," she says, looking down at our hands. "I hate to ask you to do this, but having you around does make me feel better."

I warm at that. I like that she feels safe around me. "Really, it'll be fine." I pull back. "But we will have to flirt and have some physical contact when he's around to actually sell it."

"He's the last guy I dated, and our relationship wasn't

exactly healthy, so I don't know how well I do in relation-ships." She glances down at her hands.

"Just look at me like you did when you first saw me yesterday, and I think we'll be just fine, Jules." She looks up, startled, and I give her a wink. A faint flush appears on her cheeks.

Pretending that I have to *pretend* to flirt with her is going to be fun. I've never been a natural flirt. Talking to women usually has me stumbling over my words and blushing like a little kid. But with Juliet? I've been dreaming about things I could say to get her to blush for years.

"You, uh, saw that?" she chokes out.

"You checking me out? Yup." I grin. "Like what you see?"

She gives me a little shove. "I just wasn't expecting you to be all grown up."

"You were expecting a scrawny little kid, and instead you found a man who wears glasses and is much hotter than the last time you saw him."

The blush on her cheeks gets darker, and I bite the inside of my cheek. This relationship situation we've found ourselves in might be pretend, but she can't hide that there's some obvious attraction. It's fine, but it means I've got to keep my heart locked up. I can flirt, push her buttons, make her blush, but I won't give her my heart. I can't. Because I know how it ends if I do that. I'll be crushed, and she'll be off playing soccer for one of the best teams in the world.

I bump her knee with mine. "Teasing, Jules."

She breathes out in relief. "Oh."

"Relax. It'll be fine. We'll flirt a little when we're in public and he's around. I'll hold your hand or put my arm around your shoulder. Easy peasy."

"Easy peasy," she repeats.

We go back to cookie decorating, and I'm thrown back in time to the last Christmas I saw her.

"Blair, can you come help me with the presents?" Juliet shouts through the house just as I come up from hiding in the basement. I thought she and my sister had left about ten minutes ago. I swear I heard Blair's car, since my bedroom window is right by the driveway.

"Hello?" Jules yells again.

I find her sitting in the middle of the family room surrounded by presents, wrapping paper, and bows. "Hey, Parker. Have you seen Blair? She said she was grabbing a snack from the kitchen, but that was almost fifteen minutes ago."

I sit on the couch, pulling out my phone. "Pretty sure she left about ten minutes ago. I thought you left too." I can't look at her. She's back from college for the break and has been staying here. It's killing me, but somehow she's even prettier than she was before. Her hair is longer, and she's wearing less makeup than she used to. I actually like it that way. It makes her green eyes shine more than usual.

"She promised she'd help me wrap the presents I have to drop off at the elementary school this afternoon." Jules groans. "But she totally ditched me."

She grabs her own phone and types out a text. A second later, her phone pings and I see her deflate. "She asked me if she could go to this football signing with the Cheyenne Wranglers at the mall, but I asked her to stay and help. She told me she'd be back soon, but there are probably a million people there and I don't think we'll see her any time soon. Everyone loves having a team so close to cheer for."

We live about forty-five minutes south of Cheyenne, and even though we've got the Broncos in Denver, it has been fun having a team in Wyoming to cheer for.

"She'll be there all afternoon," I say. I should go back downstairs and work on my homework. After my sophomore year of high school, when I couldn't deal with the stupid guys in my grade always making fun of me for liking math, my parents let me take classes online to get my high school degree that way. But in the past eighteen months, I've also finished my associate's degree online. If I'm lucky, I'll finish my bachelor's before I'm twenty, then I can start working at the local college as a math tutor until I can teach there. But in order to do that, I need to go do some homework, even if it is Christmas break.

"I can help you," I blurt.

She looks at me in surprise. "Don't you have friends to hang out with? A girlfriend to see?"

I hope my cheeks don't turn red. I shake my head. "All my friends go on fancy trips or visit family for Christmas. I can help."

It's dumb, really, this desire I have to be close to her. She's been in my life for as long as I can remember since she's Blair's best friend, and she's never looked at me twice. Why would she? But I'm not going to pass up the opportunity to hang out with her.

"Only if you're sure. There are a lot of presents."

"I can help," I repeat. Before sitting beside her on the

floor, I pick a Frank Sinatra holiday CD and put it in the CD player my parents insist on keeping around. I don't mind it, though; it means I can listen to what I want, when I want, without having to pay for a monthly subscription to one of the streaming platforms.

I clear some toys on the floor so I can sit and start wrapping. The nostalgic music fills the air as we cut, wrap, and tap.

"How'd you get roped into this anyway?" I ask after a while.

"I'm trying to get some more service hours. It's something my soccer team does each year to give back, and this was one of the options. I had to pick up all the donations, wrap them, and then drop them off at the elementary school by tonight since tomorrow is their last day before the break."

I look around the room. There are about thirty presents we still need to wrap, and that doesn't include the growing pile of presents she already wrapped.

"Easy peasy," I say. I can sense how tense she is, worried about getting this done on time. "We've got all morning."

Her green eyes meet mine, and I swear if I weren't sitting, I'd be knocked down. I can't remember the last time she ever looked at me like this. She smiles a little. "Easy peasy."

I nod, grab the nearest toy, and start wrapping.

"How are the two love birds?" a voice booms from behind me. I clench my jaw and Jules drops the cookie she was frosting. It lands, unfortunately, with the frosting on the table.

"Geez," she gasps. "You scared me."

We both shift to see her ex standing above us with a shifty smile on his face. "Didn't mean to startle you, babe." He leans down, his fingers touching her shoulder as he leans in real close. My blood boils, but I don't reach out. Jules isn't some prize to be won, and I'm not about to make her feel like I'm trying to lay some claim over her just because her slime ball ex is leaning over her. I would like him to step back, though.

"Let me know when you're ready for a real man again." He says this loud enough for me to hear.

"Parker's more of a man than you'll ever be," she snaps at him. This doesn't faze him.

"I'm sure he's got quite the collection of Pokémon cards," he says with another cheap smile. This guy is the worst.

"Actually, he collects Dungeons and Dragons characters; he's a dungeon master, aren't you, sweetie?" She reaches across her ex and her warm hand lands on my thigh. I swallow nervously.

"Yup," I manage to say, wondering how she knows that. I've got a group of friends that play every Friday night in the common area outside my office on campus.

"Nerd," he scoffs.

"Nerds are pretty hot," Jules says quietly. She bites her lip like she does when she's nervous, but her eyes never leave mine. "I like the slutty little glasses."

I freaking knew it. She likes the glasses. When I was in high school, I always wore contacts because they made me seem less of a nerd. But I hate having to put contacts in every day, and glasses are so much simpler.

And if Jules likes them? Well, now I'm never taking them off.

Her ex sputters. "It makes him look even more like a nerd."

I don't spare him a glance. "But at least I can see this gorgeous woman who's right in front of me. And I'm not about to let her out of my sight."

It's a subtle dig at him from what she's told me, and her eyes light up in amusement.

"Whatever," he says before storming off. But Jules stays close, looking at me, watching me. I shift, uncomfortable. I don't want her to see everything going on in my head. My parents have always said I'm an open book when it comes to my emotions, and I'm not about to let Jules read what's on my mind.

She blinks, breaking eye contact, and clears her throat. "Your glasses do look good, by the way," she says casually as she picks up a new cookie and dips her knife in the green frosting.

"Thanks," I croak.

She doesn't look at me, but there's a faint pink on her cheeks as she hums along to "Holly Jolly Christmas." I don't know what to think of anything that's happened in the past hour, so instead, I throw myself into cookie decorating, hoping it will distract me from the stunning woman beside me.

It doesn't.

Chapter 9

Juliet

We leave the sugar-scented room, and my hand is wrapped up in Parker's. I'm not going to lie, it's weird to hold his hand. Not because holding hands is funny or because it's fake, but because it's Parker.

I've known him practically his whole life but never glanced at him twice until yesterday. And now he's pretending to be my boyfriend so that Axel will leave me alone. I have no idea if it'll actually work or not, but I do know that I've got to keep my heart locked up. I can admire Parker's good looks and enjoy the hand-holding while knowing it isn't real, but I can't actually fall for him. It's a good thing I live in DC and he lives in Colorado; that'll make it easier to remind myself that none of this is real, because in five days, it'll all be over anyway. I can only hope that Axel will get the idea that I'm not ever coming back to him and that he'll leave me alone when he's back in DC too.

"Should we grab dinner?" Parker asks.

My stomach rumbles loudly. "I guess you have my answer to that."

He chuckles. "We could try that café just off the lobby. I saw some athletes eating there yesterday and it looked good. Better than the sandwiches we had yesterday."

"Sounds good," I say. We walk hand in hand to the elevator and then into the festive lobby. Down here smells like Christmas spices, but I don't know which ones exactly. All I know is that it reminds me of the mulled wine I had with Blair last Christmas when she came to visit me in DC.

The café is full of guests, some obviously athletes, while others are their guests or simply visiting the resort. We get in line and I end up ordering a grilled cheese sandwich with tomato soup. But everything looks good, and like Parker said, better than the food we got yesterday. Plus, this place is more affordable.

Parker carries our tray of food—he ordered the same as me—and I follow him to a table in the corner. We pass by a group of men, who I assume are football players. "Is that Cooper Caffrey?" I whisper to Parker. He glances over at the guy we just walked past as we sit.

"I think so. Do you want to take a sneaky picture and send it to Blair, or should I?" She's had a crush on the football star for several years now, ever since he started playing for the Cheyenne Wranglers. She'd die if she knew how close we were sitting to him.

"I'll do it," I say, but instead of taking a sneaky picture, I get up and go to his table. He's got a reputation for being a bit of a player, with a different girl on his arm every single weekend, but the tabloids also say he's nice. "Hey, Cooper, right?" I ask him.

He grins. "No way, Juliet Morgan?"

I'm surprised he recognizes me. Only avid soccer fans know my name."The one and only."

"My family loves watching soccer, so we watch you play all the time," he says. "We have to get a picture, my mom might die."

I laugh. "Well, I hope she doesn't die. But I was going to ask for a picture too. My best friend absolutely loves you."

His eyes sparkle at this. He hands his phone to one of his teammates or friends, I don't know which. He's huge, tall, and fit, but he's an athlete, which I've learned is not my type. Athletes are too hotheaded—I'm sure the same could be said about me, but I'm not trying to date me. His friend snaps a photo and then hands him back the phone. He clicks around then hands it to me.

"Here, you can send the photo to yourself."

"Only if you promise to never use my number again." I type in my number and send the photo to myself.

"Nah," he says, taking his phone back from me. "I saw you with that guy earlier at the cookie decorating. You look good together."

I grow warm. "Thanks."

"Tell your friend I say hello," he says, sitting back down.

"Will do," I say. "And let me know if your mom survives the picture."

He gives me a wide, genuine grin. "I will. She's going to freak."

With that, I return to my table, where Parker is patiently waiting. "You didn't have to wait for me. You could have started eating."

"Didn't want to be rude." He dips his sandwich in the soup and takes a bite, moaning a little. "That's so good."

I take my own bite and feel the soft bread and cheese melt in my mouth. And the tomato soup? I want to swim in it. "I think we have to eat here for the rest of the week."

"Agreed."

"You got to meet Cooper Caffrey and you didn't call me to come right away?" Blair asks weakly from where she's lying on the small twin bed.

"Can you even move without throwing up?" I ask her, plopping down at the edge of my bed, reaching for my phone, but she's still staring at the picture I took earlier.

"No, but still. I would have made it to meet him, and you didn't even give me the chance." She pouts.

"I'm sure you'll live." I don't tell her that he knew who I was since that'll just make her more jealous. "Plus, I thought things were going well with that new lawyer at your firm."

"They are. I mean, we're still in the early stages and going on dates and having fun, and she's great. But this is Cooper Caffrey. He's got the body of a god. Is he as huge and tall as he seems to be on TV?"

"He's like six-five and all muscle. So yeah," I laugh.

She groans, burying her face into her pillow. "How does it feel to live my dream?"

"Again. You'll live." I pat her leg. "Well, maybe. Is there anything I can get you? We can run to the store again if we need to."

She looks up from my phone. "Sorry you have to hang out with my brother."

"It's been fun," I say. "I mean, he's not bad company." I'm not ready to tell her that I'm kind of fake dating him, but only because I don't want to tell her that Axel is here; I don't want her to worry about me.

"Good. I am sorry, though. I'll have to make it up to you sometime."

"You have nothing to make up for," I say. "Just get better, then you can come to the ball with us."

"That does sound like a good plan." She yawns.

"I'll let you get some more rest. I'm going to go read."

"Is that what Parker is doing?" she asks.

I nod.

"We're at a resort and the two of you are going to stay in the cabin and read?"

"Looks like it," I say.

She looks like she might jump up and brave the evening, even while feeling bad, just to get us out of the cabin.

"Don't even think about it," I say. "We're fine. It's been fun, but I think we both like a little bit of quiet."

I feel a slight twinge of guilt. I know I could have signed up for more of the charity events, but honestly, I kind of just want to enjoy my vacation. I'll do the necessary activities for the charity event, but nothing extra. Maybe that's terrible of me, but it's the truth.

"You are both so boring," Blair whines.

"And you're sick. So feel better, then we'll go out." I grin at her. She settles into the bed, looking like she wants to whine about it more. "Rest. Maybe tomorrow we'll go out if you're still feeling better. Or we'll stay in again."

"Guess we'll see," she says quietly. "You letting Parker sleep in your bed?"

I really hope my cheeks don't turn red, but I feel myself get warm all over. "He said he was fine on the couch."

She chokes out a laugh. "I'm sure that's exactly what he said. But that couch sucks."

I glance in the direction of the dimly lit family room, where I can see Parker's head as he reads with a book light. "Maybe I'll go ask if he wants to sleep in the bed. Or would that be too weird?"

"Only weird if you make it weird," Blair says, yawning again.

I should go ask him, but I don't know if I will. I feel bad for making him sleep on the couch that apparently sucks, but he offered. We've already said good night. It'd be too weird to go and talk about it again. "If you're still sick tomorrow night, I'll offer again," I decide.

"Ohhkay," Blair sings. I give her a funny look, but she doesn't say anything and I can't tell what she's thinking. Does she want me to sleep in the same bed as her brother? Or does she think that's weird too? When we were kids, I wouldn't have thought anything of it. But now? I'm overthinking everything. It feels like it would be breaking too many unspoken rules of our arrangement.

When Blair doesn't say anything else, I say good night and head to my bedroom, hesitating on the threshold but going in and crawling into the bed. It's fine. He'll be fine on the couch, and if Blair is still sick, I'll ask him tomorrow night. Push a little harder. Or offer to take a turn on the couch. I pick up my book, but the words swim together on the page and I can't stop thinking about the guy on the couch just down the hall.

Chapter 10

Parker

I roll over again, hoping that maybe on this side, the couch won't feel like I'm lying on cement. But the hard cushion—if you can even call it a cushion—digs into my hip and shoulder. Sleep is futile.

I move to my back and grab my phone. May as well read or check my email if I'm not going to get any sleep. It's already one in the morning, and I've been tossing and turning all night. I could blame only the couch, but I know it's more than that.

My mind won't shut up. After Juliet and I agreed to fake date, there was more hand-holding, more flirting, and my mind is buzzing.

"It's not real," I say out loud as I pull open the email app on my phone. "Not real, just getting her ex off her back. Not real. Not real. Not real."

"You okay?"

Startled, I drop the phone and it hits my face. "Ow," I cry out.

Blair simply laughs as she appears in front of me,

wrapped in a blanket. "Do you always talk to yourself in the middle of the night?"

"Why do you walk around like you're a ghost?" I ask, rubbing my nose where my phone hit. "I didn't hear anything."

"That's because you were talking to yourself," she sing-songs.

"You seem to be feeling better," I grumble. But if she's feeling better, maybe I can get the bed back.

"I am, mostly, anyway. I think I'm past the worst of it."

"Can I have my room back, then?" I ask.

"Only once you tell me what you were talking about. Whose ex are you trying to get off your back?"

I groan. "Juliet's ex is here."

Even in the darkness, I can see how she scowls. "You'd think that her management team would have done something about that. He's bad news."

I nod. "I know."

"So how exactly are you trying to get him off her back?" Blair moves closer to me and I sit up. I'm not getting any sleep anyway; don't know why I'm trying to lie down on this horrible couch.

I clear my throat. "We're, uh, I'm pretending to be her boyfriend."

Blair cackles like this is the most hilarious thing she's heard in her entire life, which confirms the suspicion I've had all along: Jules has never looked twice at me, and there will never be anything real between us.

"Is it really so hard to believe that she'd date someone like me?" My words are gruff, but I can't hide the pain.

Her laughter stops immediately. "You like her."

Her statement hangs in the air between us. I can't deny it, because it would be a lie. But I don't want to confirm it. Jules is her best friend, and while I'm her brother, I know they have no secrets between them.

She scoots closer so she's sitting right next to me. "You really like her. Everything makes sense now."

"What makes sense?"

"Why you were so nervous to come up here. I thought it was because you didn't want to leave your routine—I know how anxious that makes you. But it's because of Jules."

"Stop," I say. I can't take this. I'm going to have to lie to my sister. "I don't like her, not like that. But her ex is a creep, and I'm here. It makes sense that I can help out."

She reaches over, squeezing my cheek as if I'm four and not twenty-four. "Always so giving, Brother. You really should do something for yourself, you know. You don't always have to take care of everything. Jules is a big girl. She knows how to handle herself."

I stand abruptly. "You think I don't know that? Of course she can take care of herself. She was the one who said she wanted to pretend we had something." I rub my hand up and down my face. I don't want to betray Jules, but Blair has to understand the situation. "You didn't see her after she saw him—she completely shut down. I'd do anything to make that better. I know what it's like to not be able to do anything because your body and mind freeze and it feels like you'll never feel normal again."

She stands too. "I was the one who went to her after

he left," she hisses at me. "I helped pick up the pieces. I know *exactly* what Axel Ashgrove is capable of."

"She froze, Blair. I had to do something."

"She doesn't need you swooping in and playing superman." She's mad, and I don't understand why. I didn't do anything wrong; everything I've done with Juliet—which has only been hand-holding—has been consensual. I'm not trying to be a hero; I don't know if I could be a hero even if I tried. How did we go from her accusing me of liking her best friend to this? "I'm not playing hero. I'm just helping. A little hand-holding when he's around, that's it."

She steps closer, eyeing me carefully, and I have no clue what she's thinking.

"Can I have the bed?" I ask. If she's feeling better, she can go back to sharing a room with Juliet and I can get some sleep.

"Nope," she says, turning on her heel and disappearing back into the bedroom.

There's a kink in my neck when I wake up the next morning, but waking up means I got at least a tiny bit of sleep. Even if it didn't happen until a couple of hours ago, I'm calling it a win.

The light is dim outside, which means I definitely didn't sleep for long, but hopefully I've slept enough to make it through the day. I take a quick shower since both ladies are still asleep, or at least both still in their rooms.

I'm reading one of my books—and actually reading—

when the door at the end of the hallway opens and Juliet appears. "Sorry, I didn't mean to sleep so long," she mumbles before stumbling into the bathroom. The door clicks shut behind her. I bite back a grin and grab my phone.

> You going to join us among the living today?

Blair texts back within seconds.

BLAIR

> Nope. Still feeling a little queasy. I'll take it easy today.

> Bummer.

> Have fun flirting with Jules ;)

> I hate you.

> You love me. And one day, you'll thank me.

> Thank you?

> Yes. You'll thank me.

> *eye roll emoji* I seriously doubt that.

I wait a few seconds, but she doesn't reply to that text. I'm tempted to go ask her what she means by that, but I don't move. The walls in the cabin are too thin, and with Blair being right across from the bathroom, I don't want Juliet to hear our conversation, even if my sister makes no sense.

"I was wondering if we could check out the gym at the resort today?" Juliet asks, emerging from the bathroom while putting her hair up in a high bun again. "My body is itching to move."

"Sure," I say. I've already showered, but I wouldn't mind lifting some weights or running on a treadmill if they have one. "Let me change real quick."

Once I've slipped into my sweats, we grab our coats and head out into the cool morning air.

"Is Blair still sick? I haven't seen her since yesterday when she was mad about me meeting Cooper Caffrey," Juliet says, pulling a granola bar from her coat pocket. "Want one?" She pulls out another one, which I take.

"She said she hasn't thrown up in almost twenty-four hours," I say and she shudders. "But she said she wants to take it easy today just to make sure she is actually feeling better."

"That's fair. I just hope we don't get it." She munches on her granola bar. "I should have woken up earlier, especially since I knew I wanted to hit the gym today. What I'd really like is to find a space where I can practice some kicks. It's been like three days since I was on the field, and that's too long."

I laugh. "You've always been that way with soccer. If you weren't playing, you got antsy."

"Did not," she says.

"Did too. Even when you were at our house hanging out with Blair, I knew you wanted to be on the field. I sometimes caught you looking at your ball and cleats longingly. Also, the fact that you brought those to our house showed exactly what you wanted to be doing."

She sticks her tongue out at me. "Most of the time I came straight from practice, so of course I had my stuff with me."

I bump her shoulder with mine. "Come on, you can tell me. You wanted to be playing still."

"I love hanging out with Blair."

"Not saying that you don't, just saying that soccer is your one true love, and I don't think anything else will ever compete with it. It's fine; I'm the same way with math."

Her head tilts up to mine, an eyebrow raised. "You know what, I was going to say that I don't think that's true. But Blair said that this is the first time you've taken an actual break in almost two years, so I believe you."

What she doesn't know is that I let math consume me. It's easier to think about math—especially when I'm focused on helping my students understand algebra—than it is to think about anything else. If I'm thinking about math, my mind can't worry about real and unreal threats. Math helps my mind stay quiet, which I like. I'd never be able to do anything if I didn't have math.

"Thanks, I think."

I see her breath in the cold air in front of us as she laughs. "It's nice to have someone in my life who also has something that consumes their every waking thought."

"And Blair's work doesn't do that?"

"I mean it does, at least a little. But she's a lot better at putting her phone or computer away when someone needs something. She's good at separating it from her personal life. Everything I do is soccer-related. Even this trip. The only reason I'm here is because I'm a soccer player and this whole thing is athletes raising funds for Winterbrook, which is cool, but it's still all part of my career."

"Does that bother you? That everything in your life is your career?" I ask as we reach the lodge. I open the door for her and she steps inside, grinning up at me.

"Thank you, boyfriend." Her eyes are mischievous.

"You're welcome, girlfriend." Two can play at this game.

She grabs my hand as we walk through the lobby. "Just in case we see you-know-who."

"Sure," I say. "But I did notice you avoided my question about your whole life being soccer."

"Nothing gets past you, huh?"

"Not when it comes to you." The words slip out, and the world slows for a beat. Two beats. She blinks up at me. I clear my throat. "Are you going to answer?"

"I think we should delve into that confession of yours instead."

I shake my head. "Nope." Not going to go there. This isn't real.

She sighs. "I love soccer more than anything. I have since I was a kid. You know that. But sometimes I wonder..."

"Wonder?" I ask as we reach the lodge's gym and use our cabin key to get in. There are a few people in here already, but since it's a little after ten, I'm not surprised that it's mostly empty. Despite the lodge being full of athletes, most athletes I know are early risers.

She slips off her coat before answering. "Sometimes I wonder if I'm missing something. I see my teammates who have partners and families and I just...I don't know, it's silly."

I hang my coat up on a hook beside hers. "It's not silly to want a family or wonder if you're missing out by not having one. Do you want kids?"

She nods. "Once I retire in a few years, I'd like to have a few kids, I think. With the right guy." A shadow flits across her face; if I hadn't been watching her, I would have missed it completely. I know she's thinking about her ex, but then she looks at me. "Do you want kids?"

My stomach twists. I don't want to lie to her, but if she wants kids, that's another reason why this wouldn't ever work out. "I'm not sure." It's not a lie; I really don't know if I want kids or not. Truthfully, the idea of having to raise a tiny human completely freaks me out.

"You'll be a great dad," she says and then steps onto one of the treadmills. I get on the one next to her.

"You think so?"

"I know so; you're so good with kids. Remember that summer when we were waiting for Blair to pick us up after the camps our high school put on? I didn't have my license yet, and Blair was who-knows-where with whatever person she was dating at the time, and there were a few kids who had to wait for their parents. I tried to play soccer with them, but none of them were interested. You came up with some game—I can't even remember now exactly what you did—but they were all laughing and having the best time that they didn't want to leave when their parents did show up."

My chest warms as I remember that. I'd been going into my freshman year, but they'd asked me to help with the math camps. Then when I had to wait afterwards for Blair to pick up both me *and* Juliet, I was in heaven.

"In all honesty," I say, looking down at all of the buttons on the treadmill so I'm not looking at her when I say this, "I saw how disappointed you were when the kids didn't want to play soccer, and I wanted to make you smile. So I tried to get them to laugh."

"You did that for me?" Her voice is all soft.

"I was a dumb teenager with a crush on his older sister's best friend," I murmur. I can't bring myself to look at her. I shouldn't have told her, but I can't keep that part of me to myself anymore. For some idiotic reason, I need her to know.

"You had a crush on me?" She sounds like this is the most unbelievable thing she's ever heard.

"Mm-hm." I hit the pace button, bumping it up so I can run. Then I hit start, going from zero to sixty in a second. Just like I did with my confession.

Thankfully, she doesn't say anything and starts her own treadmill. I try to lose myself in the run, but mostly, I wonder if I'm being a complete idiot for telling her that I had a crush on her all those years ago.

Especially since I still have a crush on her.

Chapter 11

Juliet

I was a dumb teenager with a crush on his older sister's best friend. Parker's words play on a loop in my mind with each step I take on the treadmill. And when I'm not thinking about them, I'm thinking the one thing I shouldn't even be wondering.

Does he like me now?

I can't tell if I want him to like me now because I think he's hot, or if it's some other reason that I don't want to admit yet. All I know is that he's gorgeous and now he's my fake boyfriend.

What did I get myself into?

We run for almost forty-five minutes. It feels good. My mind is clear as I step off the treadmill and have to walk a few steps for my body to get used to the stationary ground. Parker stops his machine and climbs down and takes off his glasses, lifting his shirt to wipe the sweat from his forehead. I should look away, but I can't.

His stomach is all muscle. For someone who has

never played sports, he's in extremely good shape. I don't know why I'm surprised, but his six pack looks like it was chiseled onto his body. The shirt slides down and when he returns his glasses to his face, that stupid smirk of his appears again.

"Ready to go, girlfriend."

I frown. "I feel like that's a stupid nickname. Like, would you actually call me that if I was your girlfriend?"

He thinks for a moment, looking deeply into my eyes and says, "I'd call you...skills."

My mouth drops open. There's no way he knows about *that* incident unless Blair told him.

He ducks his head to hide his smile. "I'd apologize, but Blair was telling our mom and didn't realize I was in the dining room while they were talking in the kitchen, and the story was just too good."

"You can't call me something that's named after the most embarrassing moment of my life."

He tilts his head at me. "Was it embarrassing? Because it seems to me like it's the most Jules thing you could have done."

"What does that even mean?"

He takes a step closer to me. I get a whiff of his spicy deodorant and sweat, and as much as that should gross me out, I go a little weak at the knees. "It means I know you, skills."

For a split second, I'm thrown back in time to twelfth grade English class. I'd only been partially paying attention to the lesson—my first mistake—but I *thought* the class was talking about athletic skills. I blurted loudly how my soccer skills were what got me onto the U.S. team that I'd be playing for after graduation. The entire class laughed, and my teacher informed me that my making the team was great, but in that moment we were talking about the literary skills and tools that Shakespeare had used in his comedies.

Blair never let me live it down. I swore her to secrecy, but apparently, that secrecy didn't extend to her mom. Not that I can blame her; if our roles had been switched, I would have told my mom too.

I remind myself to breathe, focusing on the present moment, which is a mistake because I breathe in more of him. "I think I liked it better when you called me 'girlfriend.'"

He tosses his head back, laughing. "Too late for that. Shall we go, babe?"

I groan. Babe is worse. A million times worse. That's what Axel called me all the time.

He notices. "Got it, skills it is."

He wraps an arm around my sweaty shoulder. "It's 11:11. Make a wish."

I look up at the large neon clock that's hanging on the wall, and it is 11:11. I close my eyes, but I'm not sure what to wish for. Eleven is my jersey number, and when we were kids—Blair and I, and if Parker was around, him too—would always make a wish at 11:11.

I wish I knew what I was supposed to do with my life. If there is more to my life than soccer. I wish—hope—that maybe there's a guy out there for me that sees me for me, and not as a famous soccer player.

I open my eyes to find Parker looking down at me.

His arm is still hooked around my shoulders, so our noses are nearly touching. "Didn't know if you still did that or not," he says quietly.

I nod. "Whenever I notice it's 11:11, I do."

He smiles, releasing me. "Told you I knew you."

My heart falters. Is that not what I just wished for? "Guess so." It's all I can manage to say.

"What's next on the agenda? Showers? Food?"

I nod. "Those both sound good." Maybe while he's in the shower I'll try to talk to Blair, and if she's still not feeling well, I'll have to call my manager, Lily. There are too many feelings happening inside my body right now. I wish I was home so I could curl up under a blanket and not think about anything for a few hours. But I don't have that luxury here, so the next best thing will be to talk it out with someone. Blair is always giving great advice anyway; that's what people pay her to do. But my feelings are also about her brother, so maybe I'll just call Lily instead.

"Earth to Jules." A large hand waves in front of my face.

"Sorry," I say. "Zoned out for a second."

"Do I need to give you the phone number of my therapist? She's really helpful." He says it so playfully, but I know he's being serious. His eyes are focused, concerned.

"I'm good," I say. A woman who's lifting beside us grunts and Parker moves in seconds, grabbing the bar so it doesn't fall down and smash her face.

"Thanks," she says weakly. "I thought I could do that much weight—guess not."

He lowers the weights into the stand. "Not a problem, just make sure when you do lifts like that you have a spotter, even if you can lift the weight. It's always better to be safe than sorry."

The woman nods, embarrassed.

Parker squats down, reaching for something on the ground—I think it's the woman's phone—when there's a loud rip. I twist away immediately to try and cover up my laughter, but it's no use. It bursts out of me, and I turn and see a huge split down the seam of Parker's joggers, showing off his blue boxers.

"Oh my gosh, I am so sorry," the woman stammers.

Parker's eyes whip to mine, where I have fixed my gaze so I'm not looking at his backside. "It's all good," he says. "These are old anyway."

He hands the woman her phone before doing a side shuffle toward our coats, his backside facing the wall.

"You look like Winona Ryder in *Little Women*," I cackle. "When the back of her dress is covered with soot so she moves along the wall."

"Very funny," he grumbles, tying his coat around his waist to cover up the ripped pants. His cheeks are red, and I bet if I reached out and touched them they'd be flaming.

"Maybe if your thighs weren't so jacked that wouldn't be a problem." I laugh. "Ripper."

His eyes blaze. "Ripper? What am I, a serial killer now?"

"Of pants, you are."

He reaches for me, pulling me into him so my arms are stuck between us, then he tickles my side. I squeal, trying to break free, which only makes him tickle me more.

"I take it back," I giggle-shout. "Let me go!"

He releases me immediately. "If you're going to call me ripper, you're going to get tickled." He's slightly out of breath. I am too.

"Fine, I'll have to come up with something else. And you should come up with a better nickname too. Jules is just fine, you know."

"But everyone calls you Jules. I've got to have something that's special."

"And skills is what you came up with? I should tickle you to get you to stop." It'd be a great idea if he weren't almost a foot taller than me and a wall of muscle. I'm strong, but I don't think I would win a tickle battle and he knows it.

"I'd love to see you try."

I run at him, but he catches me, scooping me up in his arms. "Hey, no fair."

"Life isn't fair, sweetheart. Plus, you can keep me warm on the walk back to the cabin."

"You cannot seriously think that you're going to carry me back to the cabin!" I shriek.

His hazel-brown eyes meet mine, filling me with warmth that has nothing to do with his strong arms around me. "I'll put you down if that's what you want. But if you try to tickle me, I'm picking you up again."

I slowly move one of my hands closer to his side, where I know he's always been ticklish. "And what if I tickle you now?" I ask.

He nearly drops me, trying to get away from my fingers.

"Two can play at this game, ripper." I laugh.

"You'll pay for that, skills." And with that, he chases me out of the gym, through the lobby, and into the winter wonderland that leads to our cabin.

But I'm faster.

We missed the breakfast with Santa this morning, thanks to me sleeping in. I'm usually a morning person, but I think with everything going on this week with the event, plus Axel being here, my brain needed more time to rest than usual.

After we've both showered and I check in on Blair, who's sound asleep when I peek in her room, Parker and I decide that we should go sledding, one of the activities the resort offers. But when we get to the sledding area, there are so many people.

"Should we find something else to do?" I ask, taking in the line. There are too many people for me.

"Only if you want to," he says, but he doesn't seem thrilled about all the people either.

"I'd rather go do something than stand in line to go down the mountain on a tube." While it does look fun, I'm not sure it will be worth it.

"Let's go see what else the lodge has to offer," he says, and we head back toward the lodge.

"Thanks for being such a good sport about this," I say. "I know we said that we were going to do everything on the list and all the charity event activities and everything, but..."

"It's a lot?" he asks.

I nod.

"We could go watch a Christmas movie back at the cabin," he suggests.

My heart rate slows back to a normal pace. "Watching a movie sounds perfect." I want to do everything the resort has to offer—I do. I haven't seen half of the athletes or Mr. Mynt since the VIP meet-and-greet event that first day, but I'm exhausted. I don't love being so out in the open either. I need my time to recoup, to have time to myself or with people that I care about.

Playing soccer professionally has been incredible, I love being with my team and playing the game. I love hearing the fans cheering for us in the stands. But interacting with the fans? With people? Sometimes that's just too much. And it feels silly right now that I'm feeling like it's been too much when we haven't done that much this week.

"Is *Elf* still your favorite Christmas movie?" Parker asks, breaking me out from my thoughts.

"You know it."

"It's a classic," he says.

"What's your favorite?" I ask. "I feel like I should know that, but I don't think I do." Guilt swarms my body. I don't know him as well as he knows me and I hate that. Wait, why do I hate that? I shouldn't hate that.

"The Muppet Christmas Carol," he says, oblivious to the guilt that's eating me.

"Seriously?" I ask.

"One of my favorites, but probably the best version of *A Christmas Carol* there is. I watch most of them every year. One of the professors in my department hosts a marathon the Saturday before Christmas and plays pretty much every version there is at her house. She has an open invitation to everyone she knows. Come whenever, bring a treat, stay as long as you'd like. Last year, she had a schedule of when each version would be starting so you could plan accordingly."

"That sounds like some serious dedication."

He shrugs. "It's fun. A lot of people from the department come, along with her neighbors and family. It's a day full of cozy Christmas movies and good times."

"And you're missing it this year," I say, feeling guiltier than ever now.

"It's all good. I can watch them anytime."

"But it's not the same experience. We should definitely watch the Muppet version and another if you want to," I say quickly. "I don't think I've actually seen that version." Or any version of *A Christmas Carol,* actually. My go-to movies this time of year are *The Santa Clause* and *Elf.*

"Only if you want to," Parker says, looking sheepish.

"We can have our own movie marathon today," I say. "Maybe we should go get popcorn and other treats from that store so we can stay in the rest of the day."

"That sounds great." His shoulders relax a little, and I wonder if he needs a break from festivities as much as I do. "I can run to the store if you want to figure out the TV in the cabin and if we can login to the streaming platforms or if we need to connect a laptop to it. I've got mine, and any cords we'd probably need."

This makes me smile. "Of course you do."

"I am a professor after all; gotta be prepared."

"For a movie marathon?" I ask.

He grins at me. "Always."

Chapter 12

Parker

When I get back to the cabin with all the best movie snacks, *Elf* is queued up on the TV.

"Is it okay if we watch this one first? Then *The Muppet Christmas Carol?*" Juliet asks.

"Of course." I'm not about to tell her that we could be sitting here watching paint dry and I'd be down. "But I should warn you, we're not going to make it through even one movie sitting on that couch."

Her face scrunches in concern. "What do you mean?"

"Have you not tried sitting on it?" I ask, putting the bag of goodies on the small table.

"Yes, but I guess I blocked it from my memory." She sits on the couch, adjusting trying to get comfortable. But I know she won't be able to.

"Did you get any sleep last night?" she asks.

"A little."

She stands, her eyes lighting up. "I've got an idea, but you'll have to help me."

I follow her down the hall and into the room she's staying in. It smells like her: pure vanilla. She must use a vanilla lotion or something. "What's the plan?"

"Help me move the mattress. We can put it on the floor in front of the TV and sit on it with our backs against the couch."

"I like the way you think," I say. I notice a faint blush on her cheeks, and I want to comment on it—tease her about it—but I don't want to be weird. There's no point in pretending right now since her ex isn't around, and after my confession this morning and her not saying anything at all about my old crush, I don't want to make her uncomfortable. So we move the mattress in silence, minus a few grunts from both of us as we shift it off the bedframe and into the hall, then slide it along the ground into the front room.

"What are the two of you doing?" Blair's door opens and she appears, looking the same as she did last night.

"We're going to have a movie marathon," Juliet explains. "And the couch is like the bed in my first dorm in college, which means sitting on it for even more than a minute is excruciating on your bones and body."

Blair snorts. "I forgot your first bed sucked until your mom got you that mattress topper."

"That was heaven-sent. The only reason I got any sleep that year." Juliet gives the mattress another push, and I angle it so we can set it down on the floor. "Want to join us?"

"Maybe," Blair says. "I'm gonna try to shower and see how I feel after that. You do not want me snuggled up by you smelling like I do." She raises her arm and sniffs her armpit, then grimaces.

Juliet laughs. "All right, you go shower, but we're not waiting for you to start."

"I would never ask you to. I haven't showered since we got here, so I'm going to enjoy it. I might even soak in the tub for a bit instead. So if you need to use the bathroom, now is the time to do so."

"I'm good." Juliet laughs again. "Thanks though. Enjoy your bath."

"Enjoy your movie," Blair says. Juliet turns to grab blankets, and Blair wiggles her eyebrows at me.

"*What?*" I mouth at her.

"*Go get your girl,*" she mouths back.

I shake my head. That's *not* what is happening right now. I hate that Blair now knows about my old crush on Juliet and that we're fake dating. She's always been like this when she knows I like someone, teasing me endlessly and trying to get me to make a fool of myself. Just so she can see me fall flat on my face. She loves me, I know that, but I think nothing brings her more joy than seeing me embarrass myself. It's exactly what would happen if I tried to make a move on Jules. So, it's not going to happen. We're going to go watch a movie together, but that's all.

"I'm going to make some popcorn," I declare loudly to the cabin. "And I got M&Ms, so we can put those in the bowl too."

Blair rolls her eyes. She knows that I hate when chocolate and salt mix. She also knows that Jules loves popcorn and M&Ms. "Wooing her already," she whispers.

"Nah," I say, even though I did intentionally get both those things to make popcorn this way for Jules.

"Whatever, brother." Then she disappears into the bathroom.

"What was that about?" Juliet asks behind an armful of blankets.

I grab them from her. "Blair just being my annoying older sister," I grumble.

"Is she still giving you a hard time about not wanting to come?"

I shake my head, dropping the blankets on the mattress. Juliet grabs one and starts to lay it out. "No. But she does give me a hard time about everything else in my life. I'm twenty-five, not six. She doesn't need to baby me."

The bathroom door opens. "I heard that," Blair calls out. "Not babying you, little brother, just trying to make sure you're happy."

"I am happy," I say.

"But you could be happier, have the—"

"Don't you have a bath to take?" I interrupt her. I have no idea what she is about to say, but I am positive it has something to do with Juliet, and I don't need my sister meddling in this, whatever this even is.

"Fine." Blair shuts the bathroom door again.

Juliet eyes me. "You wanna talk about whatever that was?"

"Not particularly. I'm going to make that popcorn now."

"Extra M&Ms, please." She grabs another blanket, making a nest of sorts. Gosh, if I make it through this afternoon without trying to hold her hand, it'll be a miracle.

I'm in a cocoon of warmth. I burrow deeper into the blankets. The weight I usually feel when I wake up in the morning—the one that only goes away when I'm on campus and teaching—isn't there this morning. Instead, I'm surrounded by something that smells like cinnamon and sugar and vanilla.

My eyes snap open.

Morning sun seeps through the blinds by the front door of the cabin. Morning sun. I blink again, realizing that what I'm smelling is Juliet's hair, which my face is buried in. She's curled into me, the little spoon. Sleeping soundly. My left arm is around her waist, holding her against me.

What the heck happened?

The last thing I remember was starting our fifth movie, *It's A Wonderful Life,* around midnight last night. After we watched *Elf,* we ordered some takeout for dinner and Blair joined us for movies two and three before calling it night. Jules had picked *The Santa Clause* after that, then said we should watch the ultimate Christmas classic. I remember the movie starting, and that Jules was in her own cocoon of blankets.

We laughed through some of the best parts of all the movies, talked through some of the slower parts as well.

But I kept myself in check. Absolutely no flirting—there was no reason to, with us being in the cabin and Blair watching every move I made. So how did we get from that to me holding her and breathing against her neck?

She fits so perfectly.

I hold in a groan. I should not be thinking about how good it feels to have her in my arms, to wake up like this. Or how perfectly we do fit together. I should move and get up before she realizes we were cuddling.

I breathe slowly, trying to move my arm from around her without waking her up. She shifts and I still, barely breathing now. She rolls over, pressing her face into my chest, her hands tucked up by her face on my chest, still fast asleep. There's no way I can move now without waking her up.

I hear a door down the hall open. I can't tell if it's the bedroom or the bathroom door, not that it matters. It'll be Blair.

Since I'm facing the opening of the hallway, I see her step into the room. Her eyes lock on me and Jules, and widen a fraction. She takes a step backward, turns, and heads back down the hallway. A few seconds later, my phone vibrates on the couch, where I must have left it last night.

The noise is loud enough that Juliet shifts again; her breath hitches and I know she's awake.

Chapter 13

Juliet

Maybe if I keep my eyes closed, Parker won't know that I'm awake. I squeeze them shut tighter, thankful that my face is against his chest so he can't see it. I even out my breathing, slowing it down. Maybe, just maybe, he's still asleep and doesn't know that I'm currently clutching the front of his shirt, completely nestled against him.

How much of the night did we sleep like this? How did this even happen?

I don't know the answer to either of those questions, but I do know that I don't want to move. And that's completely terrifying. I should extract myself from his arms and make a funny quip about how it was cold last night and he was warm so I must have naturally gravitated toward him. But I don't do that.

His arm is heavy around me, but it also feels safe and secure. Like he wants me tucked in next to him just as much as I want to be here. But that can't be right because he doesn't feel that way about me. At least, he doesn't seem to do anything more than surface-level flirting, and that's only when Axel is around.

But he did smirk and flirt with you even before that, remember the first day? If it's possible, I close my eyes even tighter, trying to forget that first day, when he caught me checking him out. But all I can see is his handsome face, grinning at me like he knew the secret I didn't even realize I was keeping.

I know you. The words he said yesterday echo through my brain. What if I'm not keeping any secrets and he can see my attraction on my face? What then?

I shift slightly so that I can look at his face. When I open my eyes, he's already watching me.

"It's creepy to watch people when they sleep." Why does it come out all breathy? What the heck is wrong with me?

"Wasn't watching you. Woke up when you moved." His voice is deeper, raspier than it normally is. Chills cover my skin and I shiver. He pulls me in closer to him. "Cold?"

"Mm-hm," I whisper, still staring at him. If I moved, even a little, I could kiss him right now. I lick my lips, and his eyes flicker toward the movement then back up to my eyes. He's searching, but I'm not sure what for. Should I kiss him? Would that be weird, or would it be perfect? When did Parker go from my best friend's younger brother to someone I *want* to kiss? I don't know, but right now I don't care. All I want now is to know how his lips would feel pressed against mine.

For a breath, neither of us move. His heart beat is a steady drum under my hand, making me feel alive and brave all at the same time. My gaze flickers to his lips that look so perfectly kissable. When I look in his eyes a second later, they're darker than before.

"Jules," he whispers and my belly dips.

"Morning!" Blair's voice is loud and harsh against the moment her brother and I are having, but the word does the trick, because we scramble apart, or at least we try to. But we're tangled in each other and the mountain of blankets I put on the mattress last night. "Well, isn't this cozy?"

I sit up, which isn't the best idea, because there's a blanket wrapped around my shoulder, which is also somehow wrapped around Parker, and he moves forward at the movement, his head nearly landing in my lap, which doesn't seem physically possible with how we're tangled together. We both move away from each other.

"What time is it?" I ask, grabbing my phone on the couch. There's a text from Blair.

> Guess you aren't over that old crush, huh ;)

I drop the phone, which is *not* mine. My eyes flick toward Parker, whose face is beet red.

"A little after eight. I'm feeling better though; you two want to get ready and we can go get breakfast?" Blair asks.

"Yup," I say. Is it hot in here? I feel like it's a million degrees. But that also could be because my best friend almost walked in on me kissing her brother. I have got to get a grip. This isn't a good idea. He's attractive, sure. He makes me laugh and he's the best snuggler. But that doesn't mean I can go and fall for him. How would that even work for us? He lives in Colorado and I live on the other side of the country. Nope, it's best that she walked in right before I kissed him. That would have been bad for all of us if I'd given in to those emotions.

"You and Parker looked pretty cozy together this morning," Blair says as she grabs more of the shredded white paper that we're putting into glass ornaments as snow. Parker said he had some work he needed to do, so he stayed back at the cabin instead of coming to this activity, which hurt more than I want to admit.

"It got cold last night," I say, stuffing my own ornament with paper. "We must have fallen asleep during the movie." He must have turned off the TV at some point, because the last thing I remember was the middle of *It's a Wonderful Life*.

"That's your excuse?" Blair scoffs.

"What?"

"Honey, I'd have to be blind not to see that you're attracted to my brother."

I gape at her.

"Don't play dumb," she says, grabbing a tiny snowman and dropping it into her ornament. "I saw the way you were practically drooling at him when we first got here, which, frankly, disturbed me at first because, ew, that's my brother. But then I started thinking about it, and you know, the two of you would be really cute together."

I set down my ornament. "What is going on right now?"

She smiles. "I'm giving you permission to date my brother. I still have to be the number one person in your life, but you can date him."

"Blair," I squeak. "I don't need your permission because I'm not going to date him."

"I heard you already are." She smirks and it looks so much like Parker's half smile that I have to look away.

"That's not real." I stare at the fake snow on the table in front of me.

"But you want it to be."

"How could you possibly know that?" I ask.

"So I'm right, you do want it to be real?"

I groan. "It would never work and you know that. I have my own life in DC; I'm not about to move back to Colorado. I'd never ask him to leave his work. After Christmas, we'll both be going home. And four days isn't exactly enough time to decide you want to date someone long distance."

She claps. "I knew it! And when I saw the two of you this morning, I knew it."

"What exactly did you know?"

"That you two are meant to be."

"Since when have you ever believed in anything like that? You're always telling me that dating isn't worth it and that I should just enjoy my single life."

"That was before, when you were getting over Axel. Now we could be sisters, for real."

My head spins. "Whoa, whoa, whoa. Slow down. I'm

fake dating your brother and you're planning our wedding?"

"You're getting married?" Axel appears at the table in front of me and my stomach turns sour. If he heard the first part, he'll know that my relationship is fake.

"No," I say at the same time as Blair says, "Yes."

His head swivels between the two of us, settling on me. There's hurt in his eyes, which I should ignore, but it makes my heart hurt. "I didn't realize you and lover boy were that serious. Didn't look all that serious the other day. I honestly thought you were faking it, just using him as an excuse to make me jealous so I'd be begging you to come back to me by the end of the week."

Okay, my heart doesn't hurt anymore. "It's real."

His eyes narrow at me. "Has he proposed?"

"Not yet," I say with more confidence than I feel. "But we've talked about it." We absolutely have not.

He takes a step closer to me. "Well, we'll see if he ever does, or if you come running back to me."

I shiver for the second time today, but this time, it's because I'm creeped out, not because I want to make out with Parker.

Axel reads this all wrong and gives me a slimy grin. "You'll see. Save me a dance at the ball. We'll talk then." He winks at me before walking off.

"Was he always that creepy and weird?" Blair asks as soon as he's out of earshot.

"I don't think so," I say. "But maybe I just never noticed."

"You also haven't ever dated anyone else. For the past two years, he's always been able to call and you'd be there to pick up. Maybe this is just how he acts when he's jealous. But it's still weird. And creepy."

"Agreed. It's definitely weird. Hopefully, though, he'll get the idea that I'm not interested anymore and I'm not someone he can just call when he gets bored in between flings."

She grins. "Right, cause you're going to date Parker."

"Can we please talk about something else?"

"All right, fine. But I'm not dropping this. We're going to come back to it."

"You've been sick almost the whole time we've been here, and you don't want to hear about the resort at all? Or anything else that doesn't involve your brother?"

Her eyes light up. "Okay, you're so right. Tell me everything. How was sledding?"

"That did not happen, way too many people. I kind of freaked, so we watched movies instead." Shoot. Talking about the resort isn't going to lead the conversation away from Parker at all since I've spent all my time with him.

"You're thinking about him right now, aren't you?"

"Shut up."

Chapter 14

Parker

I hide away in the cabin the rest of the day, like the coward I am. When Blair and Jules return after dinner with leftover pizza for me, I can't seem to look at Jules.

We almost kissed this morning. I'm sure of it. The way she was looking at me? I knew she wanted to. I wanted to. If Blair hadn't come in and interrupted...I can't let myself think about that. It already feels like a gut punch knowing how close I was to knowing what she tastes like, knowing how her lips feel against mine. I'm already dying from knowing how it felt to wake up with her in my arms. A kiss would have destroyed me.

"Want to watch another movie?" Jules asks, plopping on the mattress still in the middle of the room. But I don't know if I can handle a repeat of last night.

"I'm kind of tired," I say. "I was hoping to get to bed earlier tonight since we have the polar plunge tomorrow and everything. But I can help you move the bed back to your room."

"I am not letting you sleep on the couch again," she says, her eyes soft. They're melting me. I tried—not very hard, but still—to keep my heart locked up, and she broke down the walls faster than I could even blink.

"He can have the twin bed again," Blair cuts in, and I want to fall at her feet in gratitude. "I'm feeling better now, but let's keep the bed out here. I want to watch something tonight."

"Okay," Jules says, watching for my reaction.

"Sounds good," I say, hoping I look and sound normal and not like I feel. All of this is awkward. I'm making it awkward. The best thing for me to do right now is to go to bed. Maybe everything will be back to normal in the morning. "Sleep well, ladies."

"Night," Blair says, plopping down onto the mattress beside Jules, who's still watching me.

"Night," I say. Jules looks like she wants to say something, but time stretches and she looks away. With that, I head into my room and shut the door.

Her scent isn't as strong in here, since she hasn't spent much time in this room. I'm grateful for it, but also mad at myself. I should have said yes to a movie, just to spend more time with her. This is probably the last time I'll ever get to spend time like this with her. Soon, she'll be back in DC and will probably meet a nice man who can make all her wishes come true. And it won't be me.

I twist the knob. Screw it, I'm going to enjoy every second I can with the woman who's had my heart since I was fifteen. I pull open the door, stepping back in surprise when I find Jules standing in front of it.

"Thought you might want this." She holds out my phone. "Guess you realized you didn't have it."

"Uh, yeah." I swallow. No. This is all going wrong. "Thanks."

I take the phone from her, our fingers brushing. Her eyes snap to mine. Does she feel the same jolt of electricity I do when our fingers touch? I don't try to pull my phone away, and she doesn't let go. It feels like we're in some sort of weird limbo and I hate it.

I take a step closer. "Night, Jules."

"Sleep well," she says, letting go of the phone. The loss of her hand next to mine hits like a low blow. But then she steps forward, closing the distance between us as she wraps her arms around me, her head resting on my chest.

I hug her tightly, gently pressing my lips against her hair. "You too."

She steps back, cheeks pink, then nods once before turning and walking back down the hallway to where my sister waits for her.

"Are we really going to do this?" I stare out at the icy water and shiver. Both Blair and Jules look at me.

"We're doing this," they say in unison. But neither of them move to take off their coats and warm clothes.

There is a huge group of people gathered around the small lake that sits behind the resort. Some have already run and jumped into the freezing cold water and are wrapped in towels and sipping the hot chocolate that's promised to each of us once we complete the tortuous challenge. It's mid-afternoon and theoretically warmer than it was this morning, but it's still too chilly for a swim.

"Why do people even do this?" I grumble. My face is already freezing from the bitter cold wind, and getting in the water? That's not going to help anything.

"It makes them feel alive," Blair says, peeling off her coat. I don't miss how she shivers as a gust of wind blows through. Several people cry out from the cold.

"I already feel alive."

"You promised." Jules's words have me moving faster than anything else could.

"Let's get this over with then." I pull off my sweat-shirt, and I can't help but notice that Jules stares at my bare chest. I shuck my pants, revealing my bright neon-green swim trunks, which make her start laughing.

"What on earth? Those are blinding against the snow," she says, cackling.

"So? A man can't have a little bit of color in his life?" The color is truly obnoxious and opposite of what I usually wear, but when I saw them in the store over the summer, I had to have them.

Blair still hasn't moved and watches us, shivering. I turn my attention to her. "You coming, Sis?"

"Yup, just waiting until the last possible second to expose all of my skin to the cold."

Juliet's coat falls to the ground beside mine. She slips off her sweats and pulls her hoodie over her head, and I burst out laughing, doubling over. Her one-piece swim-suit is the exact same color as my trunks.

"You made fun of the color of my suit when it's the same as yours?" I gasp.

"It was from the Odette Finley collection, right?" she says. "I love her stuff; it has so much color. And I love that she makes clothes for everyone."

I nod, still laughing.

"It's insanely bright and I love it." She shivers. "And I'm freezing. Let's do this."

She holds out a hand to me, which I gladly take, loving the feeling of her warm hand in mine. Then she holds out her other hand to Blair, who's ready, standing in her dark gray swimsuit. Together, we run into the water. Jules stops short as soon as her feet touch the icy water. Without thinking, I grab her, pulling her into my arms and dragging us both into the frigid water, pulling us under.

It's a shock to the system and as we come up for air, I feel like I can't breathe. Jules wraps her arms around my neck, her entire body shaking from the cold. "Worth it?" I gasp.

Her eyes drop to my lips. "Yeah."

I pull her closer against me, but with the freezing water surrounding us, there's no way we're going to warm up unless we get out. "Let's get you warm."

She nods in agreement, and only lets go of me when I'm closer to the shore and she can stand on her own. Blair is close behind us. We run to the volunteers who have towels for each of us and wrap the thick, warm fabric around our freezing bodies.

We hobble toward the large tent that's been set up to help block out the wind so we can get our hot chocolate.

Once we do, I look around the space to find a seat. There are some tables set up, but mostly there are just benches. I find an almost empty one and tug on Jules's towel with my free hand. "This way."

Shivering, we sit on the cold bench. "Where's Blair?" Her teeth chatter as she asks. I look around the space and spot Blair talking to an athlete at a nearby table.

"Over there." I point, taking a sip of my hot chocolate. The warm liquid fills me with warmth and I take another sip, careful not to burn my tongue by drinking too much at a time. Jules is shaking beside me. I open up my towel. "Come here." She curls into me, and I wrap my towel around the both of us. I'm not super warm, but I've got to be warmer than her. She's got muscle, but she's still a tiny thing.

We sip our hot chocolate in silence, snuggled together on the bench. Life can't get better than this.

I nearly jump from shock when her icy fingers touch my thigh. "You have a tattoo?"

I look down to see part of my tattoo peeking out from the bottom of my swim trunks. "I do."

"What is it?" she asks, tracing the number one that she can see. I set my hot chocolate on the bench beside me, then tug my shorts up a little, revealing my tattoo.

"11:11?" she asks quietly.

I didn't get the tattoo because of her—not really. I got it because when I was eighteen, I felt like I needed all the wishes I could get, all the luck in the world. "I wanted a physical reminder that hey, life isn't all bad, and if I took time to make a wish, then my mind had to pause for a second, forget whatever I was spiraling over for a moment, and be present. I wanted to have those numbers on my skin to help ground me when nothing else would. I picked my thigh so no one else would see it but me, and having to move my shorts a little so that I could see it would also help ground me in reality. A tiny reminder to make a wish whenever I needed one. To stay present while also dreaming of the future."

She traces the numbers with her finger. "I love that."

"Make a wish," I whisper in her ear. I want to tell her that far too many times, I've wished for her. Not always for her and me to end up together, but I'd wish for her happiness, or for her to have a good day.

With her hand still on my thigh, she looks up at me, leaning closer. Our breath mingles as her nose brushes against mine. Can she feel how fast my heart is pounding? All it would take is for either of us to move ever so slightly, and we'd be kissing. In this tent full of people, I'd be kissing Juliet Morgan.

"Well, isn't this nice." A booming voice, which was already annoying to me but that I'm really starting to hate, sounds over us. Jules ducks into me, her face against my bare chest, and I look at Axel.

"What do you want?" I growl.

"Her."

Jules stiffens and my grip on her tightens.

"She's not some prize to be won," I spit out. "Jules is a person, free to choose who she wants to be with, and she's made her choice. If you don't leave her alone, we're going to have a big problem."

He makes no effort to move away; instead he simply

scowls at us. "Looks like she's got a man who does all the talking for her."

Juliet pushes off of me, standing to her full height, getting up in his face as much as possible. "I'm going to say this one last time, loud and clear. You and I are done. We have been for months. Leave. Me. Alone."

His eyes flare, but he takes a step back. "You're going to regret this."

She folds her arms across her chest. "I won't."

He curses before storming off.

Blair appears with an armful of our clothes, which Juliet grabs and starts putting her pants on. She's furious. I am too.

"What happened?" Blair asks.

"Nothing worth repeating," Jules says. "Nothing worth remembering."

"Are you okay?" Blair asks her.

Her eyes meet mine, and some of the fury softens. "I will be."

Chapter 15

Juliet

After getting changed—and finally getting warm—we have dinner, then head to the front of the lodge, where the sleigh ride will be. The sleighs are all lined up, each with a single lantern, driver, and horse.

"Oooh," Blair says, jumping up and down. "Look, we can roast s'mores by the fires." She points to where there are several fire pits, each surrounded by chairs and people handing out sticks and marshmallows.

"I was really looking forward to a sleigh ride," I say. "It feels like the perfect Christmas thing to do."

"Go do it, then," she exclaims. "I'll claim a fire for us, but I'm not waiting. I'm going to eat a s'more or two before you two get back."

Parker holds out an arm. "Shall we?"

I loop my arm through his. "I guess so."

I catch the smirk that fills Blair's face. She seems to want this to be real, but I don't know how it could ever be.

Parker leads us to the line of people waiting for a sleigh.

"You folks having a good time?" a booming, cheerful voice asks. I turn and see that it's Mr. Mynt.

"We are," I tell him. "It's been the best week. Thanks for putting it together."

He holds out a hand. "Juliet Morgan, right?"

It always surprises me when people recognize me. "Yes."

We shake gloved hands. "Pleasure to meet you. I'm so glad you could make it out for this. You folks coming to the ball tomorrow? I think half the town will be there. We've raised so much money for the kids in Winterbrook. Really means a lot to everyone."

"We'll be at the ball," Parker says. "And this is such a cool event—you think you'll do it again?"

"We hope so," Mr. Mynt says cheerfully. "It's been a great turnout. Can I put you down for next year, if we do host the Mynt to Make a Difference event?"

"Sure," I say. It's been fun, truly. Even if I am exhausted, I love things like this that give back to the community, whether or not I've participated in everything. But the welcome pamphlet made it clear that athletes didn't have to be at every activity the resort was hosting.

"Wonderful," he says, his eyes sparkling. This man seems to be full of holiday magic. "See you folks soon. Enjoy your ride."

Parker climbs up onto our sleigh first, then holds out his hand to help me up. It's smaller than I expected, and cozy. Parker pulls the soft, heavy blanket over our legs and wraps an arm around my shoulder. Our driver makes a noise and the horses start moving, pulling the sleigh.

With the setting sun and all of the bright Christmas lights on the lodge, trees, and cabins, it feels like we're riding straight into a winter wonderland. Like we're riding into a Hallmark movie instead of real life.

"I can't believe this is real," I whisper.

Parker's arm tightens around me. "It's real."

I turn to look at him. "Even you?"

His eyes flicker to my lips. I let out a shaky breath.

"I hope so," he chuckles. "If this is all a dream, I hope I never wake up."

I lean forward, letting our noses brush. Will we actually get to kiss this time? Or will we once again be interrupted? "What does this mean for us?"

"Don't get all practical on me now, skills." His lips skim against mine between each word. "All I know is that I like you, a lot. And I get the feeling that you feel the same way."

"Mhm," I murmur. I don't think I could say anything else if I tried.

"Then let's not overanalyze or think about anything but this moment." He tilts his head, pressing a kiss against the corner of my mouth, then moving across my cheek. "Tell me five things you can see." His voice is low and husky in the hollow of my neck, where he seems content to rest while we play this little game. Again.

"Christmas lights. Horse. Driver. White blanket. You."

He laughs, his entire body shaking. "Somebody's impatient."

I squirm.

"I've had to wait seven years for this moment," he says. "I want to take it nice and slow."

"And what moment is this exactly?" I ask, only because I want to hear him say the words.

"The first time we kiss. It's going to be the thing we tell our grandkids about." The way he's talking about us and a future together should make me feel uncomfortable, but instead, the ache to kiss him only grows stronger. "Four things you can touch or feel."

"The blanket. You. Your heartbeat." I've got one hand against his chest, feeling his heart underneath all his layers. He kisses my neck again. "You doing *that*."

He pulls his face away from me. "You like that?"

"I do."

He grins. "Good. Gotta keep my girl happy."

I smile back at him, wrapping one hand around his neck, trying to pull him closer.

"Patience," he whispers, licking his lips. Is he trying to drive me insane? He must know exactly what I'm feeling because he smirks. "Three things you can hear."

"Did you switch those last two? I swear I had to name four things I could hear last time."

He shrugs, leaning forward again and leaving a trail of kisses under my ear and across my jaw. "Maybe. I'm a tiny bit distracted at the moment to know what the exact order is. Three things."

I let out a frustrated breath. "The horse hooves." I pause, trying to listen, but all I can focus on is the trail of fire that he's leaving across my jaw and neck. I tilt my neck, giving him better access, and he growls. "Did you just growl at me?"

"You're killing me, skills."

"Yeah, well. If you would stop playing games and kiss me already, then I think we'd both feel better," I grumble. He moves a hand from my back, tangling it into my hair at the base of my neck.

"One more thing you can hear."

"You teasing me."

"Good girl. Two things you can smell."

"You. You smell like sandalwood and mint. It's the best smell in the world. It also smells like snow."

His eyes shine.

"One thing you can taste."

I'm about to say *nothing*, when he tugs me closer, our lips finally meeting. I slip both of my hands around his neck, scooting closer. His lips are warm and soft, and anything but gentle. My lips part, and his tongue skims across the surface. I moan into him and feel him smile at the sound, deepening the kiss.

He tastes like mint and something that is all Parker. I want to bottle up this feeling and take it home with me forever. As I lose myself to our kiss, the rest of the world falls blissfully quiet.

When the sleigh comes to a stop, Parker pulls away from me ever so slightly, our foreheads still touching, both of us breathing deeply.

"You." Confusion flits across his face, and I lean in and give him a quick peck. "One thing I can taste. You."

A huge grin breaks over his entire face, and I can't help but mirror the expression.

"I think I could get used to this," he whispers against my lips. "But we should probably get down so that someone else can have a turn on the sleigh."

"Do we have to?" I ask. I want to stay in this little bubble of ours forever.

He nods. "You do know that I can kiss you like that anywhere, not just in a sleigh." He nudges me, but I don't move. He ducks his head, pressing another quick kiss against my lips. "I'm never going to get over the fact that you like kissing me, so I'm never going to stop."

"Is it really so hard to believe that I like you?" I ask, pushing the warm blanket off my lap. I step down out of the sleigh and turn to face him as he steps out.

"You like me?" Gosh, he's so cute when he's like this. Hands already in his coat pockets and looking down at his feet like he's embarrassed. I step into his space.

"Against my better judgment, since I'm really not good at relationships, I like you."

"You're good at relationships, Jules. You just haven't had one with the right guy yet." He sounds so confident, I wish I could believe him. But there's still a part of me that knows that once he sees all of me, every part of the day-in and day-out of life, he'll leave, looking for something better. "Nope, whatever you're thinking, stop it right now. I like you. You like me. Let's enjoy this. We can go as slow or fast as we want. This is our relationship, ours. No one else's. Okay?"

I shake the negative thoughts from my head. He's right, I know he is. And since I fly back to DC the day after Christmas, I just need to enjoy the time we have together while we have it. "Should we go tell Blair?"

One of his arms wraps around me, pulling me into a hug. "And tell her what? That we're boyfriend-girlfriend? Is that what we are?"

"I don't know," I admit.

"We're together, how's that?" he suggests. "We don't have to label it any more than that right now. It's still new, but we're together, not dating anyone else. Kissing. Hopefully a lot."

I stand on my toes so I can press my lips to his again. His arms tighten around me, pressing me against him. If he weren't holding me up, I'd be weak in the knees. I never knew that kissing could feel like this. It was never like this with my ex. Here, there's fire.

"Ew!" The sound of a little voice breaks us apart. A little girl is staring up at us. "Mom says that boys have cooties and we shouldn't kiss them unless you're married. Are you married?"

A woman appears by her daughter's side. "I am so sorry. Lottie, you can't go up to strangers and ask them if they're married."

"Why not?" she asks. The little girl can't be more than four. Her face scrunches in disgust. "They were kissing like you and daddy do, and it's gross."

I can't help it—I burst out laughing. "Sorry, we'll keep our kissing more private."

"Thanks." The little girl smiles. "My daddy owns a lodge too. But we comes to this one for Christmas this year."

She's got a little lisp and doesn't say all of the words correctly. It's adorable. I want five of her.

"Very fun," Parker says, letting go of me and squatting down next to her. "Where's your lodge? We'll have to come visit next year."

The little girl claps. "Oh, would you really? Please! Please!"

Guess she likes us as long as we aren't kissing. A tall man with a scowl on his face appears, wrapping an arm around the woman. "Lottie, what did I say about talking to strangers?"

"To not. But Daddy, they gonna come to the lodge." The man picks up his daughter.

"Is that so?"

"Lottie just invited them," the woman says, her eyes twinkling up at him. They look like the perfect little family. The man's scowl is completely gone as he stares at his wife and daughter. Now, there's just pure love. "Give them a card."

"Did you talk to the minty guy?" Lottie asks as her father reaches into his back pocket.

This question makes him scowl again.

"Don't worry about him," his wife says. "I know you wanted to bring one of his restaurants to our lodge, but we'll find something else. Someone else. I've heard of this great little place in Estes Park called The Wednesday Café—maybe we can reach out to that owner."

I feel like we've stepped into a conversation that I shouldn't be a part of. The man hands us a card. On one side it says *Starlight Springs Lodge* and the other has a website and phone number on it.

Parker tucks the card into his coat pocket. "Thanks for this. We'll be there sometime in the next year, I'm sure."

The man nods at us, clearly dismissing us, and his wife tugs on his arm. "Let's go. I'll get the contact info for that café."

"Nice people," Parker says as the little family walks away.

"But that was so random...like what even just happened?"

He grabs my hand and we start toward the fires. "Well, we learned that boys have cooties unless you're married and that Mr. Mynt doesn't want to expand into Starlight Springs. And that we have another lodge to visit sometime soon."

"I live in DC," I say. "You live here. How is that going to work?"

Parker stops walking. "I don't know. We can be long distance. We'll make it work, take it slow. Deal?"

I'm still not fully convinced we can make it work. I've tried long distance and got cheated on. But Parker isn't Axel. "Deal." Maybe just saying that will help me feel better.

Chapter 16

Juliet

Everything about last night was absolutely perfect. I can't stop smiling today, and for the millionth time this morning, my head swings to the direction where Parker is sitting.

He's already watching me, and gives me a soft smile from his seat across the small, indoor practice space. This morning, me and some of the other soccer players are doing a mini training camp with some of the kids in Winterbrook. I think some of the funds raised from the charity event are going to help their athletic programs, which is pretty cool.

Mostly though, I'm glad we got to get away from the lodge a little bit and back onto the field.

I smile at Parker, before focusing on the girls in front of me. Five of them were assigned to me—two of them are forwards like me and the other three play different positions.

We run through a few drills so I can see how they

play. My mind, which was so focused on what it feels like to be kissed by Parker, focuses now on the girls in front of me and the game I love.

We end up doing a mini three on three game, and I give pointers to all of the girls. By the end of the hour we're sweaty, but they're all grinning.

"Can we take a photo with you?" one of them, Gabriella, asks.

"Of course," I say.

"Could you take a photo of us?" one of the girls asks one of the guy soccer players. He turns around. Axel.

Shoot.

"Sure," he says.

He and I haven't spoken since his outburst at the polar plunge yesterday. He snaps the photo and hands the girl her phone. The girls all thank me again, before heading off to find their other friends and teammates.

"Could we talk for a second?" Axel asks.

"You can have two minutes," I say. Two minutes feels generous, but I'm still on cloud nine, all thanks to Parker.

"I'm really sorry about yesterday," he says, surprising me. "I just didn't realize how much I missed you until I saw you with that guy this week."

"You mean my boyfriend?"

He winces. "I wish I hadn't messed up, Juliet. I loved you."

I scoff. "When you love someone, you don't cheat on them. Twice."

"I was dumb back then. But I've changed." He looks at me, with those puppy dog eyes that used to do so many things to my heart. But now I feel nothing. "Give me another chance."

I shake my head. "That's not going to happen. Even if I was single, which I'm not, I wouldn't give you another chance. You broke something in me Axel, and it's taken a long time to realize that I'm worthy of love. A kind where the person who's with me chooses me, every time."

He has the decency to look sorry.

"You're a good guy, and I hope for your sake you have changed. Maybe the next woman you date, you won't cheat on. But it's not going to be me."

I glance to where Parker is standing, his hands in his pockets, watching me. I can tell he's ready to come to my side if I need him, but he won't come and barge in because he knows I can handle myself. I love that with him. He lets me be me, without trying to control me.

"We didn't work," I say, turning back to Axel.

"We do though, we did work."

I shake my head. "I thought we did, too, until I learned what love really is."

He jerks his head in Parker's direction. "There's no way that nerd loves you more than I did. Than I do."

"It wasn't him that helped me learn," I say. And as I say it, I realize what I've learned in the past six months. From Blair, but also from myself. "I started to love myself. Not in a selfish way, but a way that taught me I'm valuable, just being me. And that I deserved a lot more than a guy who says he loves me, then cheats on me the second he gets bored."

He looks hurt, but I don't apologize.

"We're done, Axel. Please leave me alone." And

without another word, I walk away from him and toward the man I'm hopelessly falling for. The man who was here and ready to find my mostly healed heart, and help heal it all the way.

He gives me that soft smile again, and I grin back at him. I shouldn't be falling for him, but I am.

Chapter 17

Parker

I tighten the cuff links on my dress shirt. The Merrymynt ball is formal attire—at least, that's what Blair told me when I was packing for the trip. While it's not what I like to wear, I do have one formal outfit, which will be perfect for tonight.

"Knock, knock," Jules says, knocking on the door frame. My heart stops when I see her. She's a dream in a deep-green dress. It's got long sleeves, but it hugs her in all the right places. I want to bury my head in the crook of her neck and run my hands all over her curves. I clench my hand into a fist, trying to regain some sort of control.

"You look gorgeous." The words come out gruff.

She smiles, making her look even more dazzling, and steps toward me. "You polish up real nice too."

Her hair is down, and she's done something to it that makes it all wavy and it falls softly around her shoulders. Even in high school, she never dressed like this. I'll take every version of her, but it's going to be hard to look at anyone or anything else tonight—not that I want to. I'm perfectly happy with having her take all of my attention.

"So, will you dance with me?" she asks.

"Of course," I say. I'm about to tell her that I'll save every dance for her when her phone vibrates in her hand, again and again.

She pales as she reads the onslaught of incoming texts.

AXEL

I miss you, Juliet.

I'm the one for you. Not that nerd.

I saw how you looked at me earlier.
Please, come back to me. I'll never hurt you again.

Please, babe, you're MINE.

I pull the phone from her trembling fingers and quickly block him. "He's blocked. He can't text you anymore. You okay?"

She takes her phone back from me. "I'm mad, more than anything. I hate that he's here. I hate that he's trying to ruin everything. I thought he understood where I'm at with our conversation earlier. I'm so sorry."

I brush a curl out of her face. "Hey, none of that. You have no reason to be sorry. He's not ruining anything."

"You'll probably have to stay close all night, because if he sees me alone, who knows what he'll do."

The thought of him hurting her—in any way—ever again has my blood turning cold. "If I'm not with you, Blair can be."

"I can what?" Blair asks, clipping up her hair as she steps into the small room.

Jules holds out her phone to show her the texts. Blair frowns. "You'd better block him; that's a little intense."

"Already done," I say.

"And we'll be by your side all night," Blair says.

"I hate feeling like I need to have security with me," Jules grumbles. "I just want to enjoy the ball."

"And we'll have a blast. But no making out on the dance floor; this is a family-friendly event," Blair says.

"We're not going to make out on the dance floor," Jules says.

"Well, you were making out last night in front of all those people, so it wouldn't surprise me," Blair teases. Over Juliet's head, she catches my eye and winks. "But if you two need to sneak away or come back to the cabin early...just let me know and I'll stay away."

I clear my throat. "We're moving slow, so I think we'll be okay."

She rolls her eyes. "You can barely keep your hands off of each other, but okay."

It's true. We spent a lot of today curled up together on the couch, mostly laughing and talking, but there was a lot of kissing. I like holding Juliet's hand—and holding her in general. I just want her to be close to me.

"Well, we can dance, and that'll be great," Jules says, looking at me. "Right, ripper?"

"You're going to pay for that," I growl.

She giggles. "I certainly hope so."

"I cannot believe you ripped your pants while doing a squat," Blair laughs. "That's the best thing that's happened this trip. Besides me faking getting sick so the two of you could spend time together."

Time stills.

"What?" Jules croaks.

"The two of you needed a little assistance. I just helped move things along. We only had a few days together, and as soon as I saw you together, the way you watched each other, I knew something had to be done." Blair pulls out her phone and plays a noise. A retching noise. Jules steps back into me, her back against my chest, and my arm goes around her protectively.

"What?" This time I'm the one who's asking. "You weren't really sick?"

Blair laughs, shaking her head. "I've known about your crush for years, dude. And when her eyes lit up like a Christmas tree, I knew what had to happen. But the two of you are too slow, too in your own shells, so I had to make something happen. I just can't believe it actually worked."

I have no words right now. My sister...she...but I can't even be mad at her, because I'm holding Jules, and she wants me. But I kind of hate that it feels like we were tricked into this.

Chapter 18

Juliet

I should be mad at Blair for faking being sick, for not telling me what she was up to, for a million things maybe. But as I feel Parker's big hand around mine, I'm not mad, not in the slightest. Maybe she lied, but I'd say it worked out for the best.

Even if I don't know what's going to happen with the two of us, or how we're going to make the long-distance thing work, it feels right, and I'll never be mad at her for that.

We walk into the ballroom, which looks insanely different than it did the other day. Instead of tables set up for us to meet with fans, everything has been turned into a magical winter ball. People in beautiful ball gowns and stunning tuxes twirl around the dance floor. Everything looks and feels glamorous.

"This is stunning," Blair says, pulling out her phone from her bag. "Let me get a picture of the two of you. Then we can get one of the three of us."

Parker, whose hand hasn't left my back since we

walked into the lodge, puts an arm around my shoulders, and we smile at the camera. Once Blair takes a selfie, the three of us head out to the dance floor that's already full of people. Everyone is dressed to the nines, and even though it's a fast song, Parker pulls me close to him. I raise my arms as we dance together.

Blair groans. "You two are disgustingly cute."

"Thanks?" I laugh.

"Just don't forget me now that you're in love."

Parker stills, his eyes locking with mine. Neither of us have said anything about love—it's far too early for that. Blair continues to dance, oblivious that she just opened a can of worms that Parker and I should probably talk about.

The song ends and fades into a slower song. Parker and I sway together. "You don't have to say that yet," he blurts. "I mean, this is all new. We don't have to even talk about more than being two people who kiss."

He seems so nervous it makes me grin. "I like you, Parker. A lot. I can say that."

His shoulders relax a little under my hands. "Good."

"And I like what you said about going slow and figuring this out." I've been thinking about it for the past twenty-four hours, and I've decided that if there was anyone I was going to be long distance with, it would be him. "We'll talk all the time still, even though we're busy."

"Thank goodness for phones," he chuckles.

"We'll figure it out. In our own time, even if Blair is trying to plan our wedding."

He shakes his head. "She's gonna be the death of me."

"But hey, some of her pushing made this happen." I gesture between the two of us and his hands tighten around my waist.

"I think she'd like to take all the credit, but let's be real, this was all us."

I bite my lower lip. "Okay, you might be right about that. She just gave us more time together to figure it all out."

He leans down, pressing a gentle kiss against my forehead. "And I'll be forever grateful for that."

I close my eyes, relishing the moment. I never knew that being with someone could feel like this. Safe. Whole. It might be soon, but I can see myself falling in love with him, building a life with him. I guess time will tell if I can actually trust my gut or not.

The song ends and we pull apart. "I'm going to go find some water," I say.

"Want me to come with you?" he asks.

"I'll be good. See you in a second." I make my way toward the table full of treats and drinks. I find the water and take a slow sip, scanning the ballroom. I spot Mr. Mynt in another one of his Christmas suits and smile. I love how much the man loves Christmas. Later, he'll announce the winner of the ballroom competition. My chest aches for a moment. This week went too fast, and I didn't do everything I thought I was going to do. As I scan the room, though, my eyes land on Blair and Parker and the ache in my chest eases a little. Maybe I didn't do everything that I was "supposed" to do this week, but I wouldn't change a thing. As I walk toward the two of them, Parker's eyes scan the room and I know he's searching for me.

His smile slips when he doesn't see me. He turns again, scanning the room and saying something to Blair, and she starts scanning too. Neither of them see me until I'm right in front of them. I touch Parker's arm. "I'm right here."

His entire body relaxes. He's been more on edge than I have since Axel's texts. But so far, there's been no sign of my ex, despite his weird threats. I blocked his number, and it feels like a weight has been lifted and a chapter of my life officially closed. I'm ready to start the next chapter, with Parker.

"Dance with me?" I ask him as another slow song starts.

He gathers me in his arms. "Like I'd miss a chance to hold you."

We laugh, his eyes sparkling under the glimmering lights, and all that matters is that the two of us are here, trying, and figuring it out. Who knows what the future will bring, but tonight, we're together.

Epilogue - Juliet

One Year Later

The Starlight Springs lodge is smaller than the Winterbrook resort I stayed at last year, but it's nestled against the mountains and feels perfect for this trip.

My phone vibrates in my pocket, and I pull it out and answer. "Hey, Blair."

"Are you there? Is he there? Have you told him your news yet?"

I laugh—her words are just so Blair. "Yes, I'm here. No, I don't think he's here yet, so no, I haven't told him yet."

For the past year, Parker and I have done the long-distance thing. He didn't teach over the summer and actually came and spent a few weeks with me in DC. It's been hard, but it's also been the best. And soon, we'll be living in the same state.

"I wish I was there so I could see his reaction. Also, did you know that it's Cooper Caffrey's family that owns the lodge there? Maybe you'll see him."

"Says the woman who's engaged," I chide.

"What? I can still enjoy a good-looking man even though I'm getting married," Blair laughs. I love that she's getting her happy ending, even if it's not with the hot football player that she'll probably always have a crush on.

A car pulls into the little loop at the front of the lodge where people can park to check in. My tall, thick-thighed, slutty-glasses-wearing boyfriend steps out of his Uber, waving to the driver after he grabs his bag. I stand, watching the interaction.

"Gotta go, Blair," I say into the phone.

"Ahh! He's there! Go get your man!" Then she hangs up.

Parker takes his time walking toward me, taking me in. I do a little curtsy that makes him laugh as he pulls me into his arms, pressing his lips against mine. He's warm and tastes like mint. I breathe in his sandalwood scent as my arms wrap around his neck. I just saw him over Thanksgiving, but it's been too long.

"I missed you," I tell him.

"Missed you, too, skills."

We hug for another minute, before I shiver. "Let's get checked in. This lodge seems nice."

We head into the lobby, where a few steps lead down into a sitting area. To our left is the check-in desk. An older gentleman is sitting behind the desk. "How can I help you folks today?" he asks with a cheerful grin.

"We're here to check in," Parker says. "Do you know if the owner is around? We met him last year and would love to see him again."

The old man's face turns sad. "He's currently taking a leave of absence."

"Oh," Parker says. "Well we'll just have to come back another time to see him."

The old man smiles, but it doesn't quite reach his eyes. "I'm sure he'll appreciate that, once he's back."

I want to ask what happened, but it's none of my business.

The old man nods again. "You folks here for Christmas?"

I nod. "Yes."

"You'll love it. Even if you don't ski, we have plenty of activities here at the lodge and around town for you to enjoy. What's your name?"

He types Parker's name in the computer, pulling up our reservation. He hands us our keys and a welcome packet full of all the activities and food the lodge offers.

"You two enjoy your stay. If you need anything, I'm Guy. Feel free to call for me anytime. I'm always around."

"Thank you, sir," Parker says, grabbing our bags.

"Merry Christmas," I say, waving to the old man.

Once we've settled into our room, it's time for dinner. Parker made reservations at one of the fancier restaurants at the lodge so we could celebrate our one-year anniversary. It's also where I plan to tell him my big news.

The restaurant is dimly lit, and because we're here

right at five as it opens, we're the only patrons in the entire place. A waiter leads us to a small table next to one of the windows that looks out on the snow-covered mountains.

"Is this all right?" he asks, setting the menus in front of us.

"Perfect," I say, staring out at the view. If Denver weren't three hours from here, I'd try to move to this little town; it seems like we've walked straight into a postcard.

"I'll be back in a moment to take your order," the waiter says before leaving us alone to look at the menu.

I scan the offerings—steak, fish, and fancy chicken dishes. "What do you think you'll get?"

"The filet sounds good, and the reviews I read online said that it's to die for," Parker says.

"Maybe I'll get that too."

I set down my menu, looking straight at Parker. "So, we need to talk."

He pushes his glasses up the bridge of his nose. "If you're about to break up with me, then we're clearly not on the same page." With his other hand, he sets a small, black velvet box on the table.

I gasp.

He opens the box to reveal a beautiful pink diamond sitting at the center of a rose-gold band. My perfect ring. "Marry me."

I grin. "Yes. Yes, yes, yes." I lean across the small table, kissing him deeply. He lets out a low chuckle as we pull apart.

"Glad to see we're on the same page," he says, sliding

the ring onto my finger. It fits perfectly. "Now what do we need to talk about?"

"I hope you haven't quit your job at the university yet."

He shakes his head. "I need to finish my PhD. I'll stay there at least until then, even if we have to wait to get married after that, or be okay with a long-distance marriage."

I giggle, looking down at the shiny ring on my left hand. "Only...we don't have to do any of that."

"What do you mean?"

"You know that Denver has a new NWSL team for next season. I was waiting to tell you until I had official confirmation, but I was just asked to be on the team. I'll sign my new contract soon. I'll still get called up to play for the U.S. team, but my new home base will be Colorado."

Parker breaks into a wide grin.

"You're coming home?"

"I'm coming home."

This time, he's the one who leans over and kisses me deeply. When we break apart, I wonder where the waiter is, or if he saw us and is just giving us a minute. Either way, it doesn't really matter, because I'm coming home. But even if I weren't coming back to Colorado, I know that as long as I'm with Parker, I'll be home.

PARKER

Jules leans back in her chair, moaning. "I'll never need to eat again."

The food was delicious, but not as good as the news she told me. We don't have to be long-distance anymore. We can get married anytime. If I could go back in time and tell teenage me that Juliet is in love with me and that we're getting married, I'm pretty sure I'd fall over dead.

But it's real. It's happening.

"I have one more surprise for you," I say, holding out my hand. "Shall we?"

"You're going to have to roll me out of here. I'm stuffed." She takes my hand, though, and we head outside, where a horse-drawn sleigh is waiting for us.

"Wait, what is this?" She spins, facing me.

"I pulled a few strings." The truth is, I called the lodge weeks ago, asking if they offered anything like this for guests. I spoke with Guy, who was delighted by the idea, telling me that they'd never had sleighs, but he'd make it happen. My original plan was to propose on the sleigh, a call-back to last year when we were just falling for each other, but back at the restaurant felt more natural, more right.

Juliet's warm hands frame my face as she beams up at me. "Have I told you lately that I am absolutely in love with you?"

I smirk. "You may have mentioned it once or twice."

She leans in, kissing me, and I lose all sense of reality when her lips meet mine. She tastes like the chocolate-covered strawberries we had for dessert, and I pull her closer to me.

"I love you," she whispers as we break apart.

"Love you too," I say, resting my head against hers. "And you know, I can kiss you on the sleigh."

She smirks.

"I hope you do."

THE END

Ready to head to Starlight Springs and stay awhile? Book one releases in April 2026. You can pre-order here.

Acknowledgments

Somehow, I've made it to the end of another book. The Holiday Assist was a book that I thought (foolishly hoped) would be simple to write. I sat down so many times to write it, but the words simply would not come. In the end though, Juliet and Parker did tell me there story, and for that I am forever grateful.

Thank you to McKenna, who read (and loved) the very messy first draft of this book.

Thank you to Jana and Kristen, my incredible editors who helped make this book shine.

Thank you to Tomi, Katie, Larissa, Deb, and Michelle for the countless Zoom calls and chats while we figured out how to make this series work. I loved working with you ladies.

To my cats and dog who kept me company in my office on the long nights when I wrote and edited this book, I love you furballs.

And, to Griffin and Von, thanks for being the very best family a girl could ask for. I love you, always.

Read The Peppermint Playbook Series

Also by Taylor Epperson

Starlight Springs

Only A Game - April 30, 2026

The Nelson Sisters

The Luck of Finding You

The Rules of Mistletoe

Begin Again

RomCom Standalones

Off Trail Love

The Holiday Assist

Young Adult

Part of Forever

About the Author

Taylor Epperson has dreamed of writing books since she was a kid. She firmly believes that every story needs kissing and romance. And that every person deserves a love story.

When she's not writing, she's working in an elementary school library, reading, or hanging out with her daughter and husband. Taylor lives in Northern Colorado with her family, two cats, and one dog.

www.ingramcontent.com/pod-product-compliance
Lightning Source LLC
Chambersburg PA
CBHW021920170626
46807CB00007B/2918